Washed

Away

A Folly Tale

Vanna Byrd

CONTENTS

ACKNOWLEDGMENTS

Humbled and Thankful

Thank you to South Carolina Chief Byron Snellgrove for volunteering to share his law enforcement procedural expertise. He and Nancy have answered countless questions over the last several months to ensure that Detective Brooke Mason followed proper law enforcement procedures as she solved this cold case.

Thank you to Pam Freck who volunteered her time to be my mentor. She inspires more from my writing. Not only does she volunteer to clean up my grammatical and punctuation messes, she asks pertinent questions to inspire my plot, character and scene development. Pam's inspirational questions based on her experience at Folly give more depth to the mystery.

Thank you to Beth, Dave, Leigh, Russel, Karla, Tina, Ronnie, Carol, and Bernie for all the beach outings that inspire the settings. Our beach escapades, some documented by pictures and others, thank goodness, only in my memory, bring joy as I write stories to share back with you!

Thank you to my childhood friend, whose name I cannot mention. Well, if I do, I will be forced into the witness protection program. You know who you are! This longtime friend volunteered to offer his unique perspective, being a local. This local's family has owned property on Folly through generations. Thank you for volunteering your time to help keep the Folly perspective. Thank you for answering questions to keep the local scenes real, the vibe beachy, and Bert's Market... Well, Bert's! Thank you for being an inspiration to keep Folly pure and telling me that it's my turn!

Thank you to Toby Turtle who is a personal friend of mine and inspired the story to include his friends. If you aren't familiar with Toby, he lives on Folly Beach. You can find him on Facebook to thank him for the educational beach walks with clean ups. Obviously, he and his best friend, Vanessa, were inspirational in the plot.

Thank you to Marian and Charlie for being my daily sounding board. You inspire with your intelligent conversation, quick wit, and tidbits that feed the creative process! Thank you for the brainstorming sessions that are invaluable!

Casey and Madison, thank you for your unwavering support through the high and low tides as you ride the waves of writing with me!

1 MEGAN

The early morning air filled Megan's lungs as she stepped out of the driver's side of the Jeep. The salty air immediately triggered her imagination with thoughts of infinite waves. She could feel the rhythm of the ocean deep in her soul as she visualized herself standing on her surfboard, slightly crouched with her left foot forward, riding a perfect wave to the shore. Still dark this morning, she was elated by the absence of other cars at the wash out, happy to have sets of waves all to herself. Although she was only 23 years old, Megan had been looking out for herself for most of her life, and had not seen her parents since middle school when they had been "locked up by the law." During those pre-teen years, she began to surf couches. It had been a way of life for the next ten years as she continued to further her education. With aspirations of "surfing on to a better life," she had studied nearly non-stop to earn scholarships. The combination of making good grades, working several jobs, earning scholarships and couch-surfing had awarded herself a bachelor's degree in Biology at the University of South Carolina. Now, she was hoping that one day, couch surfing would be a distant memory, hoping that one day she would only be surfing waves. Within days, she would be earning her graduate degree from the College of Charleston. Of all of Megan's achievements, she was most proud of her upcoming graduation. Afterwards, she would be financially independent.

Free from everyone! Free to make all of my own choices. Able to live my life as I please... and have my own place.

Megan grabbed her surfboard from the top of the

Jeep, tucked it under her right arm and walked down the boardwalk towards the beach. At the crest of the dune, she paused and stood in awe at the morning sun. Although not yet visible at this time of the morning, its glow was just breaking the darkness of the horizon. Soon, its brilliant rays would extend over the infinite blue-gray water of the Atlantic Ocean.

Can't wait to be on my board… on the water… feeling the waves…

Securing the velcro leash to her ankle, she instantly transformed into her alter-ego: The Hungry Surfer Girl. She became an aggressive surfer, who could ride any wave. Now, in the mentality to eat waves for breakfast, she hurried toward the beckoning surf. Stepping down onto the sand, movement caught her eye. Looking to find the source, she witnessed a large mound of sand move to her right. Turning toward it and stepping closer, she could hear sand being flung from the edge of the dune.

"Shhh, Shhh Shhh, Shhh"

What the heck?

Her eyes adjusted to the moonlight; she could make out the round shell of the loggerhead sea turtle. Excited to see the female nesting, Megan placed her surfboard on the sand and removed her leash. Kneeling in the dune, she quietly watched in the darkness. She could hear the swish of the sand as the turtle's flippers dug a nest.

"Shhh, Shhh" The expectant mother was average size, about three feet across. Her shell was covered in sand and small shells which had landed on top as she awkwardly used her swimming flippers to dig in the fluffier sand of the dune. Inching closer, the sound became a little louder.

2

"Swish- Swish, Swish" Of all the endless mornings of surfing, Megan had never encountered a sea turtle. Instantly, she knew that it was a once in a lifetime experience. In the past, she had considered herself lucky to be the first to see the evidence of the large creatures' late-night activities. Very rarely, she had noticed the double tracks to and from the sand dunes from the waters of the Atlantic. The remaining trail of a mother's struggle across the beach sand. However, she had never witnessed a living loggerhead turtle. The experience was very different than what she expected. Megan had seen pictures of the large creatures swimming in the ocean with the brightly colored shells. Unlike those carefree snapshots, this mother was arduously digging. Flinging most of the sand onto her own shell and little coming out of the dune. Curious, but always respectful of "creatures here below". She didn't approach or disturb the mother preparing to lay over 100 eggs.

"Swish, Swish, CLANG!"

What was that? Megan now inched closer, the sound getting louder.

"Swish, Swish, CLANG, CLANG!". Careful not to startle the gentle giant, she could see the source of the metallic sound.

OH NO! The turtle had entangled itself in a beach chair. Her head was protruding between the metal leg and the frame. She was continuing to use her flippers to build her nest However, her head was entirely covered by the fabric. Essentially the struggling Momma was working blind and encumbered while continuing to remove the sand for her special deposit. The eggs, once covered in the nest, would become hatchlings in about 50 days.

"Big girl, looks like you could use a little help." Gently, Megan pushed the metal joint of the beach chair to separate the frame. With the larger opening, the turtle easily removed her head from the entanglement. Megan thought that she heard a sigh of relief as the massive sea creature resumed her motherly instincts.

"Shhh, Shhh, Shhh, Shhh" the sound of small amounts of sand being flung by her stubby flippers. Megan backed away quietly as she removed the chair and placed it into the back of her Jeep. Frustrated with humanity's negligence in caring for the beach. She began a rant...

People oughta know not to leave __anything__ on the beach! Turtles have been using this beach longer than us. Gotta do better, people!

Turtle freed, rant finished, she felt better. Felt ready to eat some waves for breakfast! Mentally, she resumed her Hungry Surfer Girl alter-ego.

2 PALMER

Two decades and three years later, Officer Brooke Mason walked like Vanna White: graceful, yet hurried and with intent, through the police station towards Palmer's office. Although she walked gracefully like Vanna, that's where the similarities ended. Unlike Vanna's tall slim body, Brooke was small in stature with curvy hips, small waist, flattish chest, and a muscular frame. Dressed in her dark blue police officer uniform, Brooke made a calm and graceful entrance every time she paid a visit to the police station. Everyone turned to look towards her. She was definitely a head turner, with her thick blonde hair pulled back into a low bun, beautiful even-toned skin, and bright blue eyes. Her face was symmetrical with wide set large eyes, thick yet well-manicured eyebrows, and naturally pouty lips. However beautiful, she was awkward, as if she didn't realize that people only stare because of her beauty. Instead, Brooke often felt self-conscious as eyes followed her in public. She had created a saying, "Glide like Vanna," to help her to imagine walking gracefully and with confidence. She used the mantra like a shield to stave off perceived public attacks and to protect herself from personal judgment. "Glide like Vanna" was her way of preparing herself to remain calm and graceful under social pressure.

Upon hearing the message earlier this morning that she would need to meet with Sergeant Palmer, she developed a pit in the bottom of her stomach. Her last hour had been spent pondering...

What in the world have I done to be called into Sergeant Palmer's office prior to reporting for my shift? Not just "sometime tomorrow", or "at your earliest convenience", but "prior to reporting to your shift." It must be something so terrible and urgent that it needed to be addressed in person and at the station.

Most of Brooke's average work day was spent on the side of Bohicket Road investigating auto accidents and completing forms near the roundabout between Kiawah, Seabrook, and John's Island. Occasionally she would need to go to Headquarters on Lockwood Drive in downtown Charleston to receive training, or to celebrate someone's retirement. Usually when entering the station, she would immediately stop to speak to Joleen, her favorite coworker. But not today. She avoided eye contact with her fellow officers including Joleen. Not wanting to get sidetracked in conversation, she just needed to get through this meeting with Palmer.

Speaking of Sergeant Palmer, usually no news is good news. Being called to his office was like being called to the principal's office. He didn't call you to give you congratulations or a pat on the back. As a matter of fact, he only called to ask an officer to "report to HQ".

Why not a text? To say that Sergeant Palmer was not technically savvy was a big understatement. Not only did he not use texting as a means of communication, he used his phone only to talk. His primary means of contact were Joleen, post-it notes, and voicemails.

"No, Sergeant Palmer does not embrace technology."

Brooke muttered to herself as she sent a text to Joleen from the parking lot. The thought of sitting outside his office, waiting to be called in after some undetermined amount of time felt unbearable to Brooke. She texted Joleen to let Palmer know that she was on the way. Joleen had given him the message to expect her momentarily, then relayed the response:

"Tell Officer Mason to come straight into my office."

A simple text to Palmer would have been much more

efficient. But he's old school.

Tapping the knuckles of her clenched fist on the door two times for a quick knock, she took a deep breath, pushed the door open and quickly closed it behind herself. Once inside the privacy of Palmer's office, Brooke's poise changed from the grace of Vanna White to that of a scolded puppy. She sat in the chair directly in front of Palmer's desk and stared at her hands in her lap with her hairline forward and her face down. She had decided that her best move was to sit quietly and let Palmer speak first. This tactic was something that she had learned long ago from her mother. Hearing her inner voice now: *"When you are unsure of what to do, just be quiet, Brookey. Whoever speaks first loses."* Whether it was true or not, it had been helpful advice throughout her life. This morning it helped to keep her mouth shut. Sometimes, the less said, the better the outcome.

As she had entered the room Palmer had looked up from his laptop, over his reading glasses and motioned his head towards the seat. Then continued to type using only his index fingers as if in mid-thought and pecked at the laptop for another 2-3 minutes. However, it felt like an eternity to Brooke as she sat in the uncomfortable "hot seat" and waited for him to speak. Abruptly, he closed his laptop, turned around, squared his shoulders and faced his chair towards Brooke. At 63, Sergeant Palmer was old enough to be her father. He was a heavy set, overweight fella with a forward head and rounded shoulder posture as if he had once been a baseball catcher and had assumed the habit of the anticipatory stance. Although photos around his office depicted Palmer as a once-muscular man, he now sat in the rolling chair with his wide shoulders not so muscular anymore. His forearms rested on his desk and a rotund belly hung over his belt. His once-brown hair was now gray and silver.

Usually if he was approached in his office, Palmer looked annoyed as if he had much more important things to do and he was being interrupted by a petty nuisance. However, not this time, not today. A pleasant look came over his face and as he looked into Brooke's eyes, he leaned farther forward and spoke in a kind, quiet voice.

"Mason, I really need your help."

Not at all what I expected his first words to be.

Relieved, she held her scolded puppy posture in the chair almost as if still waiting for the words "constructive feedback" or "disciplinary action".

"As you know, I've been on the force a long time. I've seen a lot of things, investigated a lot of crimes, put a lot of bad guys behind bars, and I feel good about what I've done in my career. But I have one cold case that's been hanging over my head for over two decades. I need your help, Brooke. I need you to take a look at this cold case. I need closure for Megan Taylor."

He pointed to the picture on his desk as he turned the frame around to face Brooke. She had noticed the framed photograph before today. However, she had always assumed that the picture was of a relative. Palmer now spoke in a strong almost emphatic tone.

"This is Megan Taylor. I've kept her picture on my desk for the last 23 years. It's a reminder about who I work for…voiceless victims like her. She was the first suspicious death case that I worked here in Charleston County. Her case was made to look like an accidental drowning. However, it was ruled a homicide by the ME (Medical Examiner). The mystery surrounding her murder has never been solved. And it haunts me every day, Brooke. I need your help. I need someone like you with fresh eyes to review the case and help me solve it."

Brooke continued to stare at the picture of the young lady with thick, brown curly hair and a large

"Hollywood smile" showing nearly all of her teeth. Megan Taylor was an obvious natural beauty. She guessed her to be in her early 20s with dark, tan skin. The victims' unusually light blue eyes were mesmerizing. Although obviously an adult, Megan's facial expression looked almost childlike in the surprise that the picture had been taken. After a brief pause, Palmer continued.

"I'm asking for a personal and professional favor, Mason. You have written on your annual evaluation every year for the last seven years that your goal is to be a lead detective on the homicide unit. I do feel that you are ready to be moved to the homicide unit. However, I'm asking you to place your professional goal on hold and instead temporarily join the cold case unit to help me solve Megan Taylor's murder."

Most people may find a request for help like this coming from a seasoned detective to be a compliment, however to Brooke it felt as if she had been horse-kicked in the stomach. Not the conversation that she had expected, her thoughts began to race.

Place my professional goal on hold? Work a Cold Case? A 23-year-old cold case? Sounds so tedious and unfulfilling. Does anybody even care anymore?

She had spent the last seven years with the police force and worked very hard to show her investigative skills, to prove herself and to set herself apart from the other candidates in her graduating class. She had worked her way up to the MAIT in the nicest area of Charleston County, the luxurious resort community of Kiawah Island.

Working a cold case felt like a definite setback instead of a promotion. Brooke looked from the picture frame back to Palmer. His expression was unlike any that she had seen on his face before. His brown eyes were gentle, kind, questioning, almost begging for help.

Brooke looked at Palmer and she found herself saying without thinking.

"Yes, I will help you. We will solve Megan Taylor's cold case."

It had been like a compulsion spewing from her lips. She could not help herself.

Why did I just agree to help with such an OLD cold case? Very little interest to me. I have nothing to gain. OMG! What was I thinking?

"Officer Mason, you just don't know how relieved I am that you're so willing to work on this case with me." Palmer, looking like a child who had just opened a present, was genuinely smiling with delight at Brooke's cooperation. Something that she had rarely seen from a supervisor.

"I've already asked Joleen to pull everything on the case: The files, the interview tapes and the boxes of evidence. She'll have a quiet place for you to work."

With that, Palmer looked down to his laptop, adjusted his reading glasses, and prepared his index fingers for typing. Looking annoyed again, he said without looking up.

"Don't report to your shift on Kiawah Island. It's been reassigned. Just start reading the files and watch the interviews. Get up to snuff on the case, report back to me this afternoon. I want to get your thoughts on this one. That's all that I have to say. Anything else that you need for your research, just let Joleen know. See you this afternoon."

Brooke stepped out of Sergeant Palmer's office in true disbelief of everything that had just transpired.

How in the world did things go from me expecting disciplinary action to agreeing to work on a cold case of over two decades?

Her head began to pound as she could feel the

low bun tightening on the back of her head like a brain sucking parasite… starving.

3 VICTORIA ELIZABETH BENNETT

Victoria stepped out of Bowens Island Restaurant holding the arm of her father as if they were exiting a wedding procession. She used the opportunity to continue to hold his arm as they stepped down the wooden stairs and onto the soft soil of the parking lot. Wearing her Golden Goose Superstar sneakers with Veronica Beard jeans and a Lilly Pulitzer off shoulder top, one might say that she was overdressed for the casual atmosphere of the Oyster Room. However, not Victoria. This $1200 ensemble was as casual an outfit as she could muster. She loved her Folly Beach time with her father. However, even as a child, Victoria knew that Folly was far too laid back, slow, casual... well, beachy for her tastes.

I adore a penthouse view. Daddy, I love you, but give me Park Ave. I much prefer the excitement of downtown Charleston where I can really see life happening.

Standing in the dappled sunlight under the canopy of live oaks beside her father, Victoria was overjoyed at having spent the last hour with his undivided attention. At 48, she was still a daddy's girl and reveled in his love. Having lost her mother before she was one year old and with no siblings, Victoria had been accustomed to getting her way as a child. Dr. Bennett had never remarried. Instead, he purposely gave his daughter all of the attention that he had been denied. He lavished her with love and gifts, but moreso, with wisdom. His most important mantra: "act like a lady, but think like a man." His words to live by!

"Daddy, can we go for a ride? Let's go to the Market in Charleston for the afternoon." Craving more attention, she was not ready for the time with her father to end.

"No, I like it here on the island."

"It will do you good to get off of Folly for a little while."

"Over the last 87 years, I've seen everything over there and it hasn't changed..., The market is full of beautiful things... of which I need none. Oh, and the skyline of 400 church steeples is amazing. I've photographed almost all of them. The horse drawn carriages, the garden tours, the ghost tours at night. Done all that! It's a 20 min drive."

"Exactly Daddy, It's only a 20 min drive."

"Why?! I didn't lose anything at the Market."

He had become quite the recluse. Not wanting to leave Folly at all. Doing all of his shopping at Bert's Market. It is true. You can find EVERYTHING at Bert's Market on Ashley Avenue which is "the rockingest grocery in town". From first-hand experience, Victoria could agree with the advertisement "Patronized by freaks, surfers, skaters, crunks, retirees, tourists, stoners, day trippers, hippies, hipsters and regular folk." It has a grill, a deli and it never closes, 365 days a year. Another advertisement, "We may doze but we never close".

"Daddy, that place is so small. Packed with everything under the sun. Last time I was there, I saw a Brillo pad, a screwdriver and Preparation-H hanging beside each other on an aisle end cap!"

"Yes, I remember! and told you that if you need those three items at the same time, it's been a BAD day!" He laughed. And she laughed with him. Her favorite sound in the world... her father's laugh. It was wonderful to Victoria's ears. She remembered a time when he freely laughed. *Back then, back before Megan died. Everything changed that day 23 years ago... For both of us.*

"That's exactly why I love it so much! Everything I need in one place!"

"OK Daddy, let's go to Bert's Market."

She used her key fob to unlock the BMW X3 and opened the passenger door for her father.

"Do you really have to open the door for me? Makes me look old... and vulnerable. Of which, I am neither. Don't you do it when we get to Bert's."

Silently, Victoria walked to the driver side of the red on black utility vehicle, opened the door and sat on the seat with her feet still on the moist sand. She started the car and Sweet Child O Mine by Guns and Roses was playing. It was their song. As a youngster, the Appetite for Destruction CD remained in the six CD changer in the trunk of the car. They listened to the entire album at least weekly for several years. She and her father would sing it as they drove from the one-way streets of the Charleston historic district, across the Ashley River, past the round Holiday Inn, over the drawbridge at James Island then out to Folly. For some reason, the locals just say Folly. Not Folly Island or Folly Beach. She was taught her prepositional phrases and other life lessons along the drive home each day.

She pulled the soft brush from her door pocket and brushed the sand from her sneakers then passed it to her father. He had also taught her to leave everything on the island, including the sand. Once the sand was back in the parking lot, they began the short trip to Bert's Market. Reflexively, she turned off the

14

speakers as she exited the dirt parking area.

Respect for people and nature when you are here. You are the visitor. Her father had said it so many times that it was now muscle memory to lower her music. They continued in silence, admiring the elevated homes along King Flats Creek. With columns and wrap around porches, they looked more Charleston style than Folly style. She stopped beside the Bowens Island Sunset View Dock. Although it was not sunset, it was an unspoiled panoramic view of the salt marsh. Every time she and her father had eaten at the restaurant, they had stopped to overlook the water at the dock. Sometimes near high tide they had seen pods of dolphins. Mommas with babies at their side peacefully gliding through the water. At low tide they had seen hundreds of scurrying fiddler crabs. Holding the large claw in front like a weapon, they were trying to impart strength as they enter and exit tiny holes in the marsh floor. Looking down at the fiddler crabs now, Victoria thought. *It's all about how you use what you have. Size doesn't matter as much as how artfully you dance with your adversary.*

She turned down the dirt road from the restaurant back toward Folly Road. Victoria began to look closely for wildlife as they drove along the puddle filled dirt road. Often, they had sighted pelicans, blue heron, or white egrets feeding along the marsh shores. The many tall palm trees gave way to scrubby oaks then only salt marsh grasses. Before returning to the main road, the drive narrowed. At near sea level, the causeway appeared path-like with rising salt marsh on each side near high tide. Her father's eyes became wide

15

looking across the spanse of salt marsh.

"Look! Do you see the osprey?!" He was pointing and waving his hands towards the bird of prey flying overhead.

"Seahawk's wingspan must be at least five feet across." The osprey narrowed in on its target swimming below. He began to glide over the water. Quietly, with wings pulled back and his talons forward, the osprey dipped half his body underwater. With his wings flapping, the osprey emerged from the marsh, out of the water and above the surface. His entire body launched out of the water, revealing his talons which clutched a barracuda. "Did you know that an osprey can capture fish equal to their body weight? I bet that barracuda weighs half his body weight. You just never know what you'll find on Folly."

4 JOLEEN

Joleen looked up immediately when Brooke exited Palmer's office and smiled excitedly the entire time that she walked across the station towards her. Brooke had a special place in her heart for Officer Joleen Byrd. Unlike some of the other experienced officers, Joleen had always treated Brooke with respect. Although Joleen was officially a police officer, she had always worked within the police headquarters. A master at coordinating the officers and relaying real time information quickly throughout the homicide unit, Joleen, at 49, had been an officer for almost as long as Palmer, 23 years. Yet, unlike Sergeant Palmer, she had gracefully learned to adapt to all of the changes in technology. Joleen was the "motherboard" for the department. In her traditional southern drawl.

"Good mornn' Brooke... Officer Mason. You dew-win okay ta-day?" Although, Joleen spoke in her slow twangy southern drawl, she was one the most intelligent people that Brooke had ever met as she was able to adapt to changes at a moment's notice and she could re-focus her efforts into a new direction without skipping a beat.

Pivot. That's what she calls it. I'm gonna need to pivot today.

Like Brooke, Joleen was dressed in a blue Charleston County Police department uniform. However, unlike Brooke, Joleen was almost 6 foot tall, with wide set shoulders with a small waist. Her very thick curly shoulder length brown hair hung in ringlets and was pushed over to the right side of her forehead partially covering the very pale skin of her face. She wore dark rimmed large-lens glasses and black eyeliner with a cat effect that accentuated her almost cobalt blue eyes. Now motioning for Brooke to follow:

"Palmer asked me to get you set up in an interview room. Said to have everything on the Megan Taylor case ready for you." Joleen stopped at the door and motioned for Brooke to step inside as she pushed her thick hair out of her face with her right hand again. Then pointed with her left:

"It's all in there. Three boxes of paper files, one box of evidence, one box of video cassette tapes." Then, turning her tilted head to make eye contact:

"This is an old case, Brooke. None of the information is in our system. This case happened before we went digital. Before social media, before DNA databases."

Brooke only nodded her head "Yes" to Jolene's first question of how she was doing and without speaking, followed Joleen into the small interrogation room.

Couldn't be more than six by six feet, Brooke entered the bleak-looking nearly empty office. The walls were light gray and without decor. Only an old dilapidated looking metal desk void of any office accessories and a swivel chair were in the room. On the top of the desk were two white file size cardboard boxes labeled in black permanent marker:

"CASE #8033564957 EVIDENCE"
"CASE #8033564957 A/V TAPES"

To the right of the desk, side by side on the floor were three white cardboard boxes labeled in black marker:

"CASE #8033564957 FILES".

Now in the privacy of the small office, Joleen pulled the door closed and faced Brooke, leaned toward her ear, and whispered,

"Something is up with Palmer today. What did he say to you, Brooke? Can't believe that he pulled you off of your normal beat to sit in this office and work on a cold case. Are you ok?"

"Still trying to figure it all out myself." She was finally able to answer, dismayed at the loss of control over her quickly changing world.

Joleen gently squeezed Brooke's shoulder with encouragement and looked into her eyes.

"Hey girl. You got this. Just take your personal feelings out of the puzzle and do your thing. Look at the facts. If you need anything, let me know."

Joleen gave a final shoulder squeeze and walked out of the room.

Now alone, Brooke immediately started to prioritize her investigation.

First, always gotta protect any physical evidence from contamination. It would be terrible to run DNA and it comes back matching Brooke Mason. OR find MY fingerprints.

She removed a pair of gloves, donned them and then removed the disposable barrier cloth from the zip bag on the outside pocket of her purple Juicy Couture Backpack. She unfolded the disposable barrier to create a 2 foot by 3-foot plastic "clean work space". Then Brooke moved the two sealed boxes of EVIDENCE and AV tapes from the top of the desk and placed them on the clean workspace. Lastly, Brooke removed her laptop from her backpack and placed it on the left side of desk.

Organized spaces create organized thoughts.

Brooke opened her laptop and created a new folder named 'Cold Cases" and created a document inside titled "MT #8033564957."

Brooke wanted to log all of the information that

she gathered today. Her brain just needed the help of bullet points to keep information organized.

I've got to work quickly and efficiently to prepare for the "up to snuff" meeting with Sergeant Palmer this afternoon. Later, if needed, the information can be entered into a local or national database.

First, she opened the box labeled A/V TAPES. Expecting to see DVDs or cassette tapes, upon removing the top to the box, she smiled in disbelief shaking her head.

"You have got to be kidding me," She muttered under her breath. "What in the heck are these?"

The cardboard file box was filled with Maxwell Hi8 MP video cassette tapes. Each labeled with a date and time, nicely placed in chronological order. However, these tapes were not standard, and Brooke knew some research would be required to be able to view the contents.

I should have known that it wouldn't be simple. Maybe Corley will know.

She snapped and sent a picture of the box's contents to her favorite videographer for the unit, Detective Corley, followed by a text:

"Help! How do I watch these?"

Detective Corley responded immediately:

only seen those once. found a box in my dad's office. you need a sony handycam and an adapter. where are you?"

"Here at HQ on Lockwood."

"otw 10 mins. bringing it"

"Ty!"

Brooke took the time to send a text to her boyfriend, Jacob. Probably still asleep in her bed, she wanted to let him know about her changing plans.

"Working at HQ today. Plan dinner without me.

Not sure what time I'm going to get out of here."

They had made plans to have an early dinner at The Crab Shack on Folly Beach after work today. Usually, her shift started at 7:00 am and ended at 3:00 pm, but depending on the timing of the last auto accident investigation and the number of cars involved, she could be back on Folly as early as 4:00pm, or as late as 6:00 pm. Brooke was very flexible with her work schedule, staying as long as needed to finish the case. Jacob found this so hard to understand. He often became frustrated that Brooke volunteered so much free time after her shift ended in completing accident investigations. His expectations were that she be changed out of uniform and able to meet him at 4 at the Crab Shack for happy hour.

Not gonna make it to Folly for happy hour. Her thoughts of Jacob were interrupted.

5 CORLEY

"Hey, Brooke. Joleen told me to find you here. What the heck are you doing at HQ today? Why aren't you on the beautiful sand beaches of Kiawah?" Corley smiled as he walked through the door to the small office.

Detective Corley, who was dressed in the same dark blue uniform, was about the same height as Brooke. The two often joked about who was the taller with both of them at about 5'6" tall. She found Corley, who was 29 and single, to be an attractive young man, with his wavy, short, sandy blonde hair with wire-rimmed glasses. However, the enduring friendship was founded on his upbeat personality which he expressed using his bigger than life facial expressions and hand gestures. He had a passion for photography and videography and was, like Joleen, one of Brooke's favorite coworkers.

"I'm working on a cold case with Sergeant Palmer."

Brooke pursed her lips and rolled her eyes still in dismay. She was resigning herself that she would be trapped in the small room, when in reality she'd rather be on Kiawah Island solving an active case.

"Yeah, a really cold one. Like how many decades old?"

"At least two."

"Really??! Mason, do you understand these are the real deal high performance 8 mm video cassettes. Like from 1990 what?"

They both looked into the box, peering at the dates scribed on the playing card size clear plastic cassettes holders.

"May 21, 1999 to be exact." Brooke answered.

"Yeah, well, the technology may be decades old, but you will be amazed and surprised at the x-ray vision capabilities of the 1998 Sony Handycam."

Corley laughed out loud, and looked disappointed that Brooke didn't get the joke. "You don't know about the Camcorders in 1998 that could see through clothing?"

She smiled in disbelief. "Are you kidding me again Corley? See through clothing? Yeah, right. It's an urban legend, right?"

"No, really. I'm not kidding. It's true. It was Sony, they had a massive recall of camcorders."

Brooke continued to question Corley's story, and silently indicated such with a tilted head and a smirk of a smile. He smiled back, looked her directly into her eyes and continued.

"Yeah, it was the night vision/infrared mode that had such detailed video, perfected to capture footage in near darkness. Fortunately, or unfortunately, the unexpected side effect was being able to see the outline of the body without clothing."

Corley was still looking into Brooke's eyes when he started professing, "It's true! Search it!"

She pressed the microphone on her phone and spoke:"1998 Sony Camcorder Recall"

Looking at the internet result, Brooke began to laugh out loud. "It is true!" She continued to briefly read words out loud:

"X-ray vision"

"See through clothes"

"700,000 recalls"

She laughed, catching herself off guard. *Can't remember the last time that I laughed. Feels good. Leave it to*

Corley. It felt good to relax and to be herself. "Corley, you're hilarious! How do you know such obscure things?! You never cease to amaze me!"

Corley, although very stoic by nature, blushed while absorbing the compliment before he changed the subject. "Not as amazed as I am that you are working on a cold case with Palmer. So, when did this happen? Why didn't you tell me?"

"I did. I mean it just happened this morning."

Corley looked at his device as he began to question her. "It's only 7:38 am. And you just found out this morning!?" Surprise came over Corley's face as he turned wide eyed then waited expectedly for more information. He was the kind of friend that always wanted the long-detailed version of her story.

Brooke began to recount her morning. "I was out for my morning jog on Folly Beach, I heard the ping of a voicemail. Listened to it when I got back to my car. He left me a voicemail this morning at like 5:30 telling me to report to the office prior to my shift at 7. When I got here, Palmer asked me to do him a favor and get up to snuff on the cold case, and told me to start immediately and that my shift on Kiawah has been reassigned."

"Why this morning? Why after all of these years? Sergeant Palmer calls you into his office this morning. Doesn't that seem odd to you?"

"Now that you point it out, it does seem strange. At the time however, I couldn't even think to ask any questions. I was in that hot seat and wanted out of it as quickly as possible." Brooke turned while holding her arm out to the side and motioned towards all of the boxes in the room. "As much as I would like to chit chat with you about the workings of Sergeant Palmer's brain, right now, I need to know how to access the Hi8 tapes."

Corley, excited to help, began to patiently explain to Brooke about the use of the 1998 Sony Handycam. "First, plug the handycam charging cord into the electrical outlet. Next, place the Hi8 video cassette into the right side of the camcorder. Then, open the left side to reveal the screen and switch the mode to "playback". Now, use the adapter to connect it to the monitor. Press the pause/play button on the handycam, then viola!"

The video began to play. However, Corley quickly paused it.

"Almost forgot! Here!"

He placed a set of department-issued headphones on Brooke's head. Next, he inserted the cable into the connector on the end of the Sony Handycam adjusted the volume - all the way down. Pressed pause/play on the handycam to restart the video. Next, Corley used his hand to place Brooke's index finger on the + volume. Leaving her finger in place to determine the appropriate volume. Brooke adjusted the volume up and down; she pushed the pause/play button to stop the video and removed the obsolete headphones.

"Corley, Thank you! I couldn't have done this without you!" Feeling confident for the first time today, she genuinely smiled at him.

Brooke learned the value of surrounding herself and appreciating people with diverse talents. She liked being with people who were vastly different.

You don't have to be an expert at everything. Just one thing, then surround yourself with people who are experts at everything else. She continued to ponder for herself. *One of life's mysteries to me is why people try to surround themselves with others who are carbon copies of themselves. Very little to benefit.*

She loved her very diverse group of friends.

"You're welcome, Brooke. I'm always glad to feel appreciated." He smiled and turned toward the door, stopped, hesitated, and turned back. "Joleen and I are going to Marina Variety Store for lunch. Leaving here at 11:00. If you could join us, that'd be great."

"Not sure. Let me see how this goes. I'm tempted, it's one of my favorites. I love the blue crab dip there. And the view over the Ashley River is fabulous. Can I let you know closer to 11?"

"So, you're saying there's a chance!" Corley and Brooke both laughed.

"Seriously, try to make it. Brooke, you can't be all work and no play. It'll be good for you to break up your work day."

"Ok, I'll try," She was already looking down at the box full of Hi8 tapes.

"So, get out of here so I can get started."

6 WASHOUT

Luckily, the tapes were labeled in black permanent marker by date. Brooke began with the oldest, with the date and time "05/16/1999 6:09 AM" scribbled on it. She placed the Hi8 MP tape into the right side of the Sony Handycam and utilized the playback mode as she had been instructed by Detective Corley, and pushed play.

The video began. The camcorder was moving around and a Ford Explorer passenger dash and glove box came into focus in the near darkness. The camera turned abruptly to focus on the back of an officer's head as he exited the driver's side of the SUV.

"Let's go!"

Turning to face the videographer, the officer looked annoyed.

"Do we really need that thing?"

First, Brooke recognized Palmer's voice; the outline of the person on video was unclear.

So, he's always been resistant to new technology,

The videographer's voice, who Brooke did not recognize began, "Yes, this is the way of the future. One day every officer will have a video camera, and it will be a more effective deterrent than a gun. Just give me a second to find the switch for "night shot mode"...

The entire video turned from near darkness to a brightly lit detailed video.

"Found it!"

'Wow, the night shot mode did make a huge difference!'
Brooke continued to view the now much more detailed video, and wondered if she would be able to see through clothing. The thought of naked Sergeant Palmer was

sickening. Letting out an audible smirk as she continued to watch, the videographer's hands are seen pulling the lever of the passenger door of the Ford Explorer and stepping into the sand beside the street. His forearms and hands are covered in small nicks, cuts and long scratches now visible in the night mode. Finally, the video comes into focus at chest height, then remains still.

Maybe a tripod? There was an ambulance, parked with lights flashing, no sirens, just quietly flashing beyond the entrance to the boardwalk. Palmer had pulled his undercover white Ford Explorer into the beachside parking near the boardwalk and secured a spot, just behind an older white Jeep Wrangler.

Brooke immediately recognized the beach. It was the narrowing of Folly Island. *That's Washout.* In contrast to the luxury resort of Kiawah Island where she worked each day, she lived on the much more casual Folly Beach. Because she knew the landscape so well, Brooke was immediately interested and leaned forward in her chair. Continuing to watch the video as the brown-haired, muscular, much younger looking version of Palmer opened the back of the Ford Explorer. He picked up the yellow crime scene tape, walked up the stairs and attached the yellow plastic tape from the wooden recycling bin to the boardwalk handrail. She noted that although the video was very good in the predawn total darkness, she could NOT see through Palmer's blue police uniform and giggled. Thank goodness!

Relieved, she watched as the much more agile, slimmer version of Palmer now hurried down the boardwalk and stopped under the covered pavilion. The videographer walked towards Palmer and stopped beside him. The camera angle turned toward the beach. From this vantage, Palmer and the videographer could see the body on the edge of the shallow surf. The victim was lying on her back parallel with the water line, dressed in a pink and black wetsuit with a surfboard several feet from her on the beach. Palmer began to attach the yellow crime tape to the boardwalk railing and down to the surf at Washout to protect the area around the victim.

We don't want the tide to wash away this poor victim or the evidence at the scene.

The videographer spoke into his two-way radio. Police code for "human dead body" found. "On scene, four-one-nine confirmed." The video stopped.

Officer Brooke Mason was hooked. No longer feeling sorry for herself for being trapped in the small room, but instead feeling intrigued by this cold case mystery at Washout.

7 RYAN

Brooke picked up the next Hi8 MP tape with "05/16/1999 6:28am Ryan Willis Interview" scribbled on it and placed it into the right side of the Sony Handycam. She selected playback mode and then pressed the triangle play button.

The video focused on the face of a young, blond-haired guy with sun-kissed skin. He was speaking to someone off camera. "Yeah man, came down to pick up a few swells this mornin', an came up over ta top of the dune...Dude, she was just lying there... in da water...like, face down. Totally freaked me out...didn't even walk down there, I just called 911." Ryan was shaking his head side to side, looking down at his bare feet on the boardwalk. His long blue wetsuit covered his entire body except for his feet, hands and head. His dry hair was slapping his tan face in the beach wind.
He looks in anguish, as if he could barely get the words out of his mouth. Poor guy.

"Where was the victim when you found her?" It was Palmer's voice from off screen.

"She was floating in the edge of the surf, face down in the flats about halfway between the two jetties." Ryan was pointing with his right hand across his body to a location off camera.

"The flats?" It was the videographer's voice.

"Yeah, the part of the water that's flat after the white wash from the crashing wave."

"So, you moved her?" Palmer's voice.

"So yeah, the 911 operator kept insisting that I go down there on the water and check on her. It was obvious to me with her face underwater and all that she

30

was already toast. But I went down and rolled her over to see her face and sure enough she was dead. Totally dead." Ryan's bottom lip was now quivering. The video continued silently focusing on Ryan's distraught face for several seconds.

Off camera, Palmer pressed for more information. "What happened next?"

Ryan paused for a moment then began, "So, I backed up, came up to the boardwalk at the dunes, and waited for somebody to get here."

"So, Ryan, where did you touch the body?"

"Yeah, the woman on da phone made me do it."

"Can you show me where you touched her?"

"On her shoulder, like I said. She was faced down in the water and I used both hands and I pulled really hard on her shoulder and rolled her towards me."

"Which shoulder?"

"Her left shoulder. I put both of my hands around her left shoulder and pulled up really hard and she flipped over onto her back. It was obvious that she was dead."

Now leaning against the wooden boardwalk railing, Ryan stared down at the boardwalk shaking his head side to side again, his arms hugging himself, and his eyes wide in dismay. He occasionally looked up to Palmer as he spoke.

"So, she was face down in the water? How deep was the water?" It was the videographer's voice.

"I don't know, man. She was floating... I'm thinking halfway to my knees." Ryan pointed to his calf and indicated about a foot of water. Then continued. "But I'll tell you the weird thing. When I walked up to her, the surfboard was up on the sand, not connected to her ankle by the leash. She didn't have her leash attached by the velcro around her ankle. Why would she

31

be in the water at high tide without her board?"

Brooke, now engrossed in Ryan's interview, thought to herself: *good point. If she was here to surf, why wasn't her surfboard in the water? And surfing without a leash is prohibited on Folly Beach. It's mandatory to attach your leash. Plus, who wants to chase the surfboard around without the leash?*

"Is that why you're here at this crazy hour? High tide?" The videographer asked from behind the camera.

Ryan turned toward the camera with big eyes and a momentary flash of a smile while nodding his head. "Yeah! It's the Trifecta. High tide, full moon, and a west-bound storm formed over the ocean. Doesn't happen often." He quickly lost his smile as he turned back to face Palmer.

Palmer's voice asked from off camera. "Can you identify the victim? Did you know her?"

"Yeah, I seen her around Washout. Her name's Meg. Don't have a last name."
Ryan paused thoughtfully for a moment. "The locals used to call her the "hot surfer chick." Then as we got to know her, she became "Meg, the hot surfer chick".

Chick. Really? What a terrible word. Who uses a word like that?

As if hearing her thoughts 24 years in the future, Ryan quickly turned toward the videographer. "Hey, no disrespect by the word 'chick'. Meg is…" Ryan began to tear up, he covered his eyes with his right hand, and began to shake his head side to side. After a short pause, he resumed: "Meg was the most graceful, most muscular and best-looking wave rider. Because Meg was so wicked on her board, she became known to the surfers of Folly Beach. She was totally beautiful and totally talented. Looked like a walking advertisement for the beach. You know what I mean? Hawaiian Tropic or somethin'. No one knew her name at the time. So, she got the nickname 'hot surfer chick'." Ryan tilted his chin to his chest, crossed his arms and looked down at his bare feet. Without further prompting, he started to talk again. "Every mornin' I knew she'd be here... out riding her board at high tide... without fail. One of those things I took for granted...Seeing her, you know. Recognized her wetsuit and surfboard from the dunes. But when I flipped her over, I knew for sure it was her. Meg, the hot surfer chick of Folly Beach."

Palmer asked, "Ryan, do you know anything else about Meg?"

"Yeah, she's like a student, downtown at COC."

"C of C?"

"Yeah, College of Charleston."

"You mean that you suspected that it was Meg before you saw her face?"

"Yeah. Saw her Jeep when I pulled up to Washout and thought she'd be out already riding some waves. Jealous, you know, that she made it out on the water before me."

"You said that's her Jeep up there, show me which one." Palmer walked from the boardwalk down the steps and onto the sand. He motioned for Ryan to come down the stairs and to lead the way to the Jeep. The videographer followed.

Ryan stopped beside an older white Jeep Wrangler. "Yeah man, this is Meg's Jeep. Seen her getting in and out of it many times. Her board on top."

Brooke noted that the Jeep was without doors or a hardtop. *Either Megan Taylor lives on the Island or she uses the Jeep locally. Even the locals don't drive down the interstate without doors or tops. Jeep has surfboard racks. Definitely a local. Brooke made a mental note.*

As soon as the thought crossed Brooke's mind,

she heard Palmer's voice as if they were sharing the same thoughts over 23 years apart. "Do you know if she lives on Folly?"

"Not sure man. But she's definitely a local. Here almost every day."

Palmer looked down into the Jeep and pointed to the flip flops on the passenger side floorboard. "Was anybody with her? Does anybody else come with her?"

"Nah, man. She's always alone." Ryan continues. "Me too… Always on the water alone."

"Stay here, just another minute. I gotta make a phone call." Palmer said as he walked a few steps away from the side of the Jeep towards the back. He took out a notepad and scribbled the license plate number down.

Brooke paused the video, activated her laptop, and added a few bullet points. Although it was obvious from the video that the full name of the victim was not known at the time, Brooke had the luxury of knowing. *I guess that's one perk to working a cold case.*

Megan Taylor
Hot surfer chick
Folly Beach
Found near Washout May 16, 1999
Ryan Willis 911 caller
Student College of Charleston?
White Jeep Wrangler
SC tag SEJ 521

Brooke noted that the sticker on the license plate had expired at the end of the month in April. The day of the video was Thursday, May 16. Brooke added to her bullet points:

"Expired Tag April "

She resumed watching the video: Palmer turned around and took a few steps back to Ryan, who was now leaning against the parking voucher machine.

"You really gonna tow her Jeep? Don't you have respect for the dead?"

Palmer was quiet for a moment, then looked carefully into Ryan's eyes as he spoke.

"Yeah, Ryan. I'm going to tow her Jeep to protect it. You know, from damage or theft. Plus, I want to see if there are any clues in there. You can understand why I wouldn't want something to go missing from inside. I want to keep Meg's Jeep safe."

Ryan's expression changed from anger to belief. After a short pause, Palmer began to question Ryan again. "Tell me, Ryan, you said that you had seen Meg surf?"

"Yes, almost every day for the last two years."

"Is she any good?"

"Yeah. She's strong, good control of her board, competitive you know, willing to out-paddle you if you try to take her wave."

"So, Meg was a strong swimmer?"

"Yeah, I asked her once: How did you get to be so fast on the water? Said that she was on the swim team and a lifeguard on Kiawah at the resort.

She told me that she grew up in a mobile home without air conditioning in Red Bank Creek in the middle of South Carolina. She said that there is never a breeze there. She said that she couldn't even recall one breeze. Ever. And that it was over 100 degrees and 95% humidity on most summer days. She would walk a mile to splash in the cold water of the creek. But she had to be able to swim faster than the poisonous cottonmouth snakes that lived in the creek." Ryan trailed off and his face appeared in deep thought about Meg.

"Sounds like Meg was a strong swimmer." Palmer's voice asked.

Brooke, having the advantage of knowing that

Megan's death had been ruled a homicide, understood that Palmer's line of questions was trying to determine if Megan's death could have been accidental or intentional.

"So, she was a strong swimmer in the ocean, too?"

"Yeah, she was a strong swimmer. Mentioned something about being a lifeguard for years over at the resort on Kiawah Island. I can't believe that she drowned. Just doesn't make any sense to me."

8 BURGESS

Walking quickly through the fluffy white sand on the beach side of the street, a short man whose windblown hair was reminiscent of Gene Wilder's Willy Wonka entered the camera frame walking towards Palmer and Ryan. He wore a wide nylon strap attached to a camera. It was the size of a small baby clinging to his chest like a proud papa. The attached cone-shaped lens protruded at least eight inches out, daring anyone to approach into his personal space. His camera had a massive light attached to the top making the combo almost big enough to cover the man's entire chest. He walked straight into the frame of the recording video camera, and stood beside Palmer.

"Whatcha think, Palmer?"

That's the videographer's voice. Detective Brooke Mason's brain kicked into gear.

Now, focused intently on the video, she heard Palmer project his voice with authority.

"First, get a video of every inch of the beach. Lucky for us, tide is going out, waves are lowering on the beach over the next couple of hours... Gives us a little more time on the scene before everything is washed away. Second, get stills of this Jeep and everything around it. We believe that it belongs to the deceased. It does have an expired tag and an outstanding parking ticket, so I will call for a tow truck. It's roped off now, I don't want to lose any potential clues. Something just feels wrong about this one. It feels like foul play... staged to look like a drowning accident. I don't want to make the mistake of not collecting potential evidence and checking this one out."

Palmer tilted his head to the side and spoke into his radio as he squeezed the PTT (push to talk) button.

"Joleen, SC license tag# SEJ 521."

"10-4."

"Tow truck for said vehicle."

"10-4"

"Joleen, send the detective unit."

"10-4"

"Jolene, ETA of the coroner?

"Coroner Burgess has arrived on scene."

Video ends.

Brooke was surprised that all of the interactions between the detectives were caught on video as well. Obviously, the Sony Handycam had been placed on a tripod beside the Jeep Wrangler. She continued to watch on playback mode:

Video resumes

Coroner Burgess stepped out of his white Chevy SUV, which was parked next to the ambulance. As he walked into frame, he continued towards the recording camera, obviously now placed on a tripod.

Wow! He's tall! He looks different...His hair is darker... and longer. Look how tan he is... especially for May.

He said in a whisper as if unaware that the video camera was documenting his secret: "Listen, I drive my issued car everywhere on the island. It's easier and faster to get around with the number of tourists this time of year. They see the coroner's car in the rear view and they just move otta my way." Then, in a work voice, the coroner said,

"What do we have?"

The much younger Palmer begins: "Called in at 5:49 am by a surfer. All I know is a female potential drowning victim. ID'd by the caller as "Meg, the hot surfer chick," potentially a student at the College of

Charleston. She was found face down in about a foot of water this morning. Her surfboard was nearby on the dry beach and her leash was not attached to her leg."

Video ends.

9 VIDEO EVIDENCE

Jerky and bouncing, the video panned left to right from the dunes, across the beach, then to a rock jetty. As the video stabilized, it also blurred into focus on two silhouettes moving on the beach. Brooke recognized the figures as young Palmer and Coroner Burgess walking side by side across the near black sand. The video panned to the dark ocean, where the videographer could see the sunrise over the horizon. He zoomed in and back out.

"Come on, you're making me sick. Stop playing with every button. It's not a new toy!"

Realizing that she was talking out loud to someone who documented the scene decades ago, she chuckled to herself. *Focus. Both of us.* As if the videographer could hear Brooke from 23 years in the future, he returned to his documentation of the crime scene.

The video panned back to the beach where a female body in a black wetsuit with pink trim was resting, obviously lifeless. Her right arm was outstretched towards the surf and her left lay flat near her side. Sand was caked against the left side of her body from the ebbing tide. Although she had been found in the water by the 911 caller, she was now resting on reflective, wet beach sand giving the impression of an oil slick as the tide had continued to recede.

The videographer moved closer to the body, and Brooke could now see the victim's face for the first time. Her hair was a mass of a tangled braid that partially covered the swollen, pasty looking skin of her face. Her eyes were frozen open in a look of shock.

What happened? What are you trying to say...? Brooke paused the video to look for clues.

Poor girl, different from her picture in Sergeant Palmer's office... Her entire face was swollen, especially her lips and protruding tongue. Called petechial hemorrhage, the whites of her eyes were blood red. Brooke could see dark shadows on her neck.

Could be ligature marks. Definitely asphyxiation. She pressed play to resume the video.
From off camera, Brooke recognized Palmer's voice again.

"Going to be hard to get prints. Her fingers are waterlogged."

"We'll get them when her fingers dry out a little." Burgess was shining his flashlight on the victim's hands. "Come get a look at this!" The videographer zoomed for a close-up of her shriveled hands.

The index and middle fingers of her right hand were at odd angles at the knuckles. Her fingernails, although short, were broken and jagged.

Coroner Burgess' voice interrupted Brooke's thoughts. "Victim is Pronounced dead... he looked at his digital watch and noted the time... at 6:47 am." Using his flashlight to illuminate her body, the coroner began to describe his visual findings. "Index and middle fingers of her right hand are swollen, indicating that this injury occurred pre-mortem. The nails of all four fingers and thumb are broken."

"Defensive injuries?" Palmer's voice

"No shit, Sherlock. Looks like she put up a good fight."

"Yes, it does. We just don't know who or what she was sparring with..." Palmer made it official. "Due to the suspicious nature of the death, we are going to declare this a crime scene."

Brooke paused the video and added the clues to her growing list:

Megan Taylor

Hot surfer chick of Folly Beach

Found near washout May 16, 1999

Ryan Willis 911 caller

Student College of Charleston?

White Jeep Wrangler

SC tag SEJ 521

Facial Edema

Petechial hemorrhage

Fingers swollen with broken nails on right hand

Video resumes: Brooke could hear the sound of strong winds against the microphone. The sunrise is peeking over the horizon in tones only of black and white. The video focused on the body of Megan Taylor, laying on her right side, facing away from the videographer. The curved black silhouette of her body in contrast to the straight line of the horizon and the bright vertical light rays of the rising sun, the black and white video changed instantly to the vivid red, orange, and purple of the sunrise reflecting from the sky over the ocean, ripples of brilliant colors in the waves and wet sand.

"Hey! Look! Turn this thing on." It was Palmer's voice again. He was waving his hand in front of the lens with excitement in his voice.

"Get over here. Can you see this? Here in the sand?"

The videographer turned the camera toward Palmer's pointing hand. Disturbances in the otherwise smooth flat beach sand, contrasting details now made visible by the rising sun. Palmer continued to enthusiastically point to the beach sand that had been disturbed.

"Are you getting this? Are you getting this?"

Brooke paused the playback.

Looks like a struggle, obvious footprints and drag marks and kicked up clumps of dirt. Yes! There was definitely a struggle. Megan did not enter the water alone! Someone DID force her down the beach!

Brooke resumed the video:

Palmer continued to direct the documentation of the scene from a distance following the trail of drag marks in the sand towards the dune. The videographer started to turn away from the dunes and back towards the beckoning sunrise. However, Palmer motioned him back.

"You're still getting this, right?"

Now standing at the base of the sand dunes, Palmer was pointing to the sweet grass that had broken off at about 2 ft from the ground. Just behind the broken sweetgrass, there was a small clearing with several sets of indentations in the sand, as if someone had been standing. The footprints were indistinguishable in size or shape.

Nothing to identify the creator. However, they did indicate weight shifting in the small clearing just behind a patch of sweetgrass.

The videographer paused and focused in and out as Palmer reached into his pocket, withdrew a one-dollar bill.

Brooke, still watching the video...

Oh! to give size perspective to... Wait, that's the photographer's job. Shame on... wait, what's his name? Can't remember...Doesn't matter... So glad that I work with Corley, fella has his act together...

Next, Palmer pointed to a hole in the sand about the diameter of a quarter. And held the one-dollar bill beside it. "About the size of a broom or shovel handle. Be sure to get this." Palmer now used his index finger to show the 1" depth of the hole, careful not to disturb the sand.

"Looks like a ghost crab hole to me." The videographer's voice again as the sand came into focus.

"Look there's another one." Palmer pointed to another hole in the sand the same size but about 2 ft from the original, and a third.

"Look, it's an equilateral triangle." *Meaning the holes form a triangle with three sides of the same length.*

Palmer continued to squat down beside the holes in the sand.

"Are you getting all three of them? Young Palmer turned to look directly into the camera and emphatically stated,

"No, not ghost crab holes. These holes go straight down only an inch, not angled like the ghost crab. Not sure what the holes ARE, but they are NOT ghost crab holes."

Yeah, ghost crabs angle the entrance of their hole to create a "front porch" to keep out the water.

"Look!" Palmer said excitedly. He took out a glove from his uniform pocket and pointed to a green plastic bottle nestled in the sweet grass of the sand dune.

"Maybe we can lift a print from this." Palmer didn't touch the green plastic bottle as he instructed,

"Get a close up! Bag it as evidence, dust it for prints." The camera focused on the nearly empty 20 oz Mountain Dew bottle with the cap intact.

Fingerprint or DNA. That Mountain Dew bottle is gonna solve this case.

"Holy Moley! Mountain Dew to the rescue!" Brooke's thoughts had escaped her lips until she was called back to the 1999 video with the sound of Palmer's voice.

"Look!" The young version of Palmer enthusiastically followed the footprints away from the three holes in the sand towards the boardwalk. The footprints ended just in front of the stairs of the boardwalk. Up ahead lay the covered pavilion.

Brooke pondered, *someone else was on the beach this morning. But what were they doing?*

At 11:58 am, still deep in thought, Brooke was surprised by Corley's voice.

"Begging for you to go to lunch. We're thinking about the Marina Variety Store…"

Smiling, standing in the doorway with his elbows flexed and palms together.

He looks so handsome when he smiles.

"We? Who's going to lunch?"

"You, me, and Joleen. We gotta talk to you."

"As much as I'd love to go to lunch, I'm still knee deep in this case. Let's go to California Dreaming later instead."

"They're not open for lunch during the week… Weekdays they open at 4:00pm. I can't wait that long to eat lunch! And you know how "hangry" Joleen gets when she doesn't eat!"

"Don't expect you to wait… You two go ahead."

"You two go ahead and do what?" Joleen had just walked into the now "crowded office."

I'm asking you and Corley to meet me at California Dreaming later."

"Living on the department dime. Do you really think we can afford to eat out for lunch and dinner?" It was Joleen.

Brooke knew that it was a rhetorical question. She didn't answer, instead she looked to Corley to solve the "hangry issue".

"Okay Joleen, let's grab something to tide us over… What time do you want to meet?"

"I'll text you after I have my "up to speed meeting" with Palmer."

"Ok, this doesn't even sound like a "yes" to lunch anymore… If he's long winded, it could be a midnight snack." Brooke could tell that Corley was obviously disappointed.

"Yeah, not sure what time but I can text you. I'll meet both of you at the marina."

"Sounds like a lot more fun!" Joleen obviously was not disappointed in the change in location. Her expression became more serious and a look of concern came over her face before she began to whisper.

"About Palmer. Something's up for sure." Joleen was now standing between and just behind Corley and Brooke in the makeshift office.

"I'm really worried about him. I know that he's a gruff and tough guy but he has a heart of gold. I'm thinking something is wrong."

"Yeah Brooke, did he tell you anything about the meeting in the morning?"

"No, what is it about?"

"Palmer says there's a department meeting with all detectives at 08:00 am tomorrow. You know, at shift change so that we all have to attend, so it's gotta be some kind of big announcement."

She rewound the video to watch it again, from the beginning playing back in 25 percent speed: Video started with Megan Taylor's side-lying body, curves of her hips and shoulders silhouetted in dark shadows of sharply contrasting light and dark against muted light gray beach sand. Centered behind the contrasting silhouette was a brilliant semicircle of bright white. Sunrise! The only sounds audible were the loudly whipping wind and the lightly crashing waves unchanged, with the transformation with the press of the "night mode button". Abruptly, the video changed to a full spectrum of color. Nearly every color visible to the human eye was being emitted from the sunrise: orange, red, and purple reflected off of the ocean water and off of the clouds in the sky. A beautiful sunrise revealed all of the bright colors to provide just enough light to see Megan's body, then reflected colors of the sunlight in the wet sand highlighting the crests of shimmers of the outgoing tide.

This videographer was capturing an almost artful moment. It was creepily beautiful with the sunrise and silhouette of Megan. This artful moment was interrupted by Palmer's voice. As instructed, the videographer followed the sand disturbances to the broken sweetgrass on the dunes, then the three holes in the sand, the green Mountain Dew (Brooke noted the change in the logo from the 1999 full spelling to today's Logo Mtn Dew), and the footprints away to the steps at the boardwalk.

Now Brooke's brain was working hard. She was feeding the imaginary starving parasite inside the low bun on the back of her head.

Someone was waiting…
Behind the sand dunes,
In the sweetgrass,
Drinking a Mountain Dew.
Megan was surprised,
In an instant her life was
washed away.
Based on this information. I'm assuming that the beach
was the scene of the homicide. Two people struggled down the

beach. One person walked back up from the surf. What made three holes in the sand? They walked away...

Leaving broken sweet grass, a Mountain Dew to the rescue!

It had to have been within moments of Ryan's 911 call. Could it have been Ryan? What's his motive? How? If not Ryan, who?

Brooke started a Find and Interview List. Hopefully, Officer Joleen Byrd will be willing to help to find this witness from so long ago.

He may be hard to find. Being a surfer 23 years ago is not a great lead to locating Ryan Willis today. Maybe some of the paper files will have a last known address or employer.

Brooke glanced toward the boxes stuffed tightly with file folders and papers. *Ok, another video. Not ready to dive into deciphering detective documents from decades ago... Brooke was expecting the handwriting to be challenging. After all, she had never officially learned to write cursive... She, of course, could read it...sometimes.*

10 DOCTOR ADVICE

"Brooke, I want to go through my notes to give you a first-hand account of that morning's notification of death." Without warning, Sergeant Palmer was entering the doorway to Brooke's makeshift workspace. He was holding a chair in one hand and a file folder in the other.

"Detective Mason, before we talk about the notification of death to Dr. Bennett, I'm gonna give you some off-the-record kinda pointers… Whether the person called 'Doctor' is a MD or a DO or a PHD. Begin to think of the title as a warning. Almost everyone who has attended college for that many years should have to inform the other person that they are professionals at debate. Some people with the title may require that others use it. I've been interrupted and corrected when addressing someone as Mr. or Miss in the past. The word 'doctor' does not itself indicate the subject studied. However, it does clearly state a higher level of intellectual or social status.

I like the warning of the title. It helps to know how best to proceed to get the most out of an interrogation… interview, I of course mean conversation."

Brooke remained quiet, intently listening for Palmer's insights on detective work. She considered him to be a mentor. Pleased to have his wisdom, Brooke leaned closer as if saying, "More please."

Palmer continued with his next tidbit, "Now here's another thing. If you just want information, keep it casual, just start a conversation. Like you just want to get to know someone. The more genuine the better. On the other hand, to get the most out of an interview, make it formal. Start with announcing the date, time and personnel present for the interview. Doing this lets the person know that you are serious." Brooke shook her head 'yes'. Finally, she spoke: "All ears here. Anything else?"

"One more thing. People know that you mean business when you interview them here at headquarters. If you want to make someone relax, meet them somewhere they choose. If you want to make 'em sweat, meet them at headquarters. You won't believe the difference that a change in setting makes for those tightlipped arrogant types."

Quickly slapping the file on the desk in front of Brooke, she jumped at the abrupt sound then read the folder: Notification of Death
Megan Rose Taylor
May 16, 1999
Brooke waited to hear Palmer's recollection of the notification of death that happened so long ago.

Meanwhile, back on Folly, Victoria Bennett and her father, Dr. Bennett inspected the under-side of the newly-constructed Edwin S. Taylor Folly Beach Fishing Pier. The two strolling arm in arm along on the beach in the shade of the pier, passed the bait/tackle shop. "Wonder if they have anything worth a darn?"

Victoria knew that her father was becoming more critical of everyone and everything around him. She knew that he was about to criticize every detail of the pier. Knowing that a list of poignant statements was on the way, but she didn't care. She loved the strolls today, as much as she enjoyed their time together as a child. Victoria leaned into her father, hugging his arm. He began, "I read all about it." It was said as if it now deemed him an expert on all things Folly Fishing Pier. "They have a bathroom. Do you need to go to the ladies' room? Because, there are no facilities of any kind at the end of the pier."

"I'm good. Don't need to go now. Daddy, I'm not a child."

"Just saying. It's over 1,000 ft to the end of the pier. And you know what I always say, 'If you have the chance, why not empty your bladder and go pee?'"

"Okay. Let's stop in the Gangplank Gift and Tackle Shop and check out the bathroom." Based on past experience with her father, Victoria knew they would be inspecting every detail of the newly opened tourist attraction. *Why not start with the restroom?*

"We can stop at the restroom then get some ice cream." Dr. Bennett was delighted with his own idea, his face lit up like a father trying to enjoy time with his five-year-old child.

"No, Let's get a seat at Pier 101 and get a Folly Bubble instead."

"A what?" He crinkled his face.

"Let's go to the bathroom, wash up, then get a table. I'm ordering a Folly Bubble to sip while I overlook the water. Meet you at Pier 101."

"Whatever makes you happy, dear. You know that I love you more than anyone else on this Earth?" He hugged Victoria as if he hadn't seen her in years. Squeezed her tightly for several seconds. He let go and walked towards the public restroom. Just before he walked inside the door, "You do know about the saltwater fishing here? I'll tell you all about it over lunch." He walked through the door, out of sight. Victoria made her way to Pier 101, sat at a table overlooking the ocean waves, and ordered an adult beverage to pass the time while waiting for Dr. Bennett to complete his inspection.

11 PALMER'S NOD

Palmer's flashback of Dr. Raymond Bennett's home 08:14 AM on May 16, 1999:

A middle-aged man was standing in the framed space of the double doors. Initially with a friendly smiling face and a "Good morning!" he quickly turned to a look of shock to see two police officers at his door.

Palmer began: "I'm Detective Ron Palmer with the Charleston County Homicide Unit."

"Oh no! Is Victoria ok? Please tell me that she's ok." His voice started to crack and tremble as he steadied himself against the doorframe.

"Dr. Bennett, I'm here about a 1992 Jeep Wrangler registered to you," Palmer began again.

"Oh, so yeah, what about it? It's a YJ by the way. You know, the ones with the square headlights. Did Megan get that many parking tickets that you had to pay me a visit this time?"
Palmer's face remained calm and did not react to the jab that Dr. Bennett had just thrown. Instead, he tried to gently guide the conversation for the Jeep owner to connect the dots.

"You were aware that she was using the Jeep this morning? So, what is your relationship to Megan?"

"Yes Megan, she is a close friend. She uses the Jeep almost every day. How much are the parking tickets?"

Dr. Bennett reached towards his back pocket as if to remove his wallet. Detective Palmer handed his card to Dr. Bennett as he spoke in a very calm empathetic tone:

"As I mentioned, I'm here on behalf of the Charleston County Homicide Unit. Dr. Bennett, may we come inside?" A look of horror came over Dr. Bennett's face. Realization began to set in as he moved his hand from his back pocket to take the business card from Palmer that something had happened to Megan.

"Oh no! I mean Yes, come inside. Is Megan ok?"

From the large plantation front porch, Detectives Palmer and Wainwright stepped inside the large open front room. Although it was still early in the day, the room was filled with light from the long windows overlooking the beach. Glass dominated the Eastern wall of the room, which was almost monochromatic: white walls, tan leather sofa, ivory covered furniture, white washed dining furniture and light pine wood floors.

"Please have a seat." The composed Dr. Raymond Bennett motioned towards the dining table chair. After all, three were seated, Palmer was the first to speak. He spoke clearly while directly facing the still processing man. *The last thing you want to do is need to repeat a notification of death.*

"As I said, Officer Wainwright and I are here related to a Jeep that's registered in your name… We believe the driver of the Jeep to be deceased. We have been told that the driver's name is Megan." A look of sheer terror came over Dr. Bennett's face. His contorted look of shock was likened to someone from a Hitchcock flick.

Palmer patiently waited for his face to quit convulsing before he asked a question: "Do you have a last name for Megan?"

"Taylor, Taylor's her last name. But it can't be Megan. What happened? Did she have an accident? She can swim like a dolphin. Goes surfing every day. Couldn't be Megan."

Wait, never said a word about Megan's cause of death. Denial? First stage of grief?

Delivering a Notification of Death is very difficult. Being a good investigator requires patience with people who are having the worst day of their life. There are many stages of acceptance. In most cases they are quite unprepared for the news that an officer must deliver. However, a good investigator must learn the art of offering empathy while gathering evidence. Brooke noted that Palmer had been careful not to mention the exact cause of death.

"Do you have any contact information for Megan? We want to notify her next of kin and ask for a positive ID at the morgue."

"Can't be Meg. It can't be true. I love Meg so much." Dr. Bennett's voice trailed off and his face froze: mouth open, eyes wide and forehead furrowed.

"Are you involved with Megan in a relationship?"

"No! No! Not like that." Dr. Bennett shook his

head from side to side. With tears in his eyes, he explained:

"Megan's like a family member to us. Her parents are a casualty of crack cocaine abuse. You remember Nancy Regan's 'Just Say No" campaign? The endless commercials about 'This is your brain on crack'? Congress was able to pass the Anti-Drug act of 1988. Changed the penalties for drug distribution to be more severe than for murder. Both are currently serving 30-year prison sentences for manufacturing and distribution of crack."

Dr. Bennett excused himself to somewhere in the pantry, then came back with a box of tissues. With his hand now shaking, he placed the box on the table. He took a clean tissue, sat back down at the table across from Palmer and continued his story.

"I met her over two years ago. Megan applied for and was awarded the Bennett Foundation scholarship at the College of Charleston for postgraduate students performing research to further Exercise Sciences". Graduating from the University of South Carolina with a BS in Biology and with a 3.75 GPA was no easy feat. She was an exact match of what the foundation wanted in a candidate: intellect, ambition, and financial need. However, it was the interview that won her the scholarship. During her final response, she told the board of directors that she had been couch surfing since she was 12 years old. Just before she started middle school, her parents had been incarcerated. Without blinking an eye, Megan asked the foundation members if they hold her parents' actions against her. She pointed her finger at each of the five members and vowed: "If this scholarship is awarded to me, you will not regret it. I will not let you down... If you have further questions about my ability or commitment to the research, I will be glad to answer them now."

"It was a drop-the-mic moment... It worked. We unanimously voted her the recipient of the scholarship." Dr. Bennett appeared to be remembering a much happier time in his life as a quick upturn of his smile appeared then immediately disappeared as his thoughts returned to this moment. Taking note of the change in expression, Palmer gently asked for more information.

"So, Megan was the recipient of the scholarship. Is that the nature of the relationship?"

"Well no, we were closer, much closer." Dr. Bennett took a deep breath and began to explain their living arrangement.

"She lives here with us. Not in the main house, of course. You see, when Dr. Bob Bathe informed the foundation that Meg was homeless, we offered her a work study in exchange for rent. Meg has been our family beach house manager. She lives in the small efficiency apartment below the main house."

"Beach house manager?"

"Yeah, our extended family owns this house in the form of a trust. A beach house requires lots of maintenance. The salty air, you know. We allowed her to live in the efficiency apartment under the family beach home in exchange for her services."

"What kind of services?"

"Household Management services: scheduling lawn care maintenance, cleaning between visitors, ensuring that the family teenagers don't destroy the place, organizing and preparing different family events including catering, entertainment, guest list, among other things. "

"So, you are saying that the relationship was professional between you and Megan Taylor?"

"No, Megan is much more involved in everyday aspects of the family. She has become like a second daughter to me." Dr. Bennett broke down into a complete blubbering mess. Placing his forehead on his folded hands on the dining room table, he began to loudly sob.

Brooke, 23 years later, sitting in front of Palmer, listened intently as he finished the story of the death notification and began his assessment of the interview.

"He did appear to be genuinely shocked at the news of Megan Taylor's death. And his grief appeared to be real...however, something just didn't seem right. I found it very strange that a single older man would offer his home to a twenty something stranger. I don't know, it just seems like there is more to the relationship. I regret that I didn't follow my gut instinct back then. When you start out as a detective, it's hard to tell the difference between your gut and indigestion. Trust your gut, Mason. You have good instincts! Now, let's hope that you have good intestinal fortitude." Finally, he stopped talking and peered down at Brooke.

"Wonder if Dr. Bennett has more to say about

Megan's death. It's been 23 years since that interview."
Happy for the lead, Brooke added another name under
her Find and Interview list:

Dr. Raymond Bennett.

*Shouldn't be hard to find him. Doctors of all types have
electronic paper trails that make them easy to find. Usually, a
quick internet search will yield at least a phone number and
address of his last known medical practice. Hopefully Joleen can
help find and get him to HQ for an interview.*

12 PHYSICAL EVIDENCE

Brooke, now weary of watching videos, decided to open the evidence box. She glanced at her phone. *Oh my gosh, that took up so much time! Still so much to do and I've got to make a decision about lunch. Let me at least get through the evidence box.* She broke the seal on the cardboard lid of the box, then she removed a large, clear 5 mm thick plastic bag filled with a black wetsuit. Leaving the pink trimmed wetsuit in the evidence bag, she examined it. *I wonder if there is any fiber or DNA evidence on her wetsuit?*

Another sealed plastic bag contained a nylon cord attached to a Velcro strap. *Ok, the leash for her surfboard is obviously significant. Otherwise, why would they have kept it?*

Next, she removed three sealed clear sheet protectors: The first contained an acceptance letter from the College of Charleston, the second a scholarship award letter from the Bennett Foundation, and the third a job offer letter from Dr. Bennett.

No green plastic Mountain Dew bottle? What the hell? That's one of the only pieces of physical evidence. How else can I prove the identity of the murderer? Definitely gonna write Mountain Dew on my list of things to ask Palmer about this afternoon. Mountain Dew to the rescue.

13 PALMER'S
MOUNTAIN DEW

Palmer began: "Okay, I'm telling you first. Announcing it tomorrow. Keep a lid on it until then. Going on medical leave for a total knee replacement. Going to be out for six weeks. Are you up to speed on Megan Taylor's case?"

Now glad to have the bullet points saved on the case, Brooke opened her list and began:

"Megan Taylor, 24-year-old student at the College of Charleston found on Folly Beach at washout, face down in the flats on May 16th 1999 found by Ryan Willis, fellow surfer at 5:49 a.m. known to the victim."

"Interview Dr. Bennett - Bennett Foundation scholarship. She was living underneath his home using his Jeep and was the property house manager."

Brooke moved her gaze from her notes to Palmer, "The biggest question that I have is, where's the Mountain Dew bottle? Did you get a print from it? Where is the print?"

"Officer Mason, this is exactly why I keep Megan's picture on my desk. The Mountain Dew bottle was lost. Somehow it came up missing. Officer Wainwright went back to bag it and it was gone. It was never recovered. We never received a fingerprint from the bottle nor have it to use for DNA. Megan's picture on my desk is a reminder to always inspect what I expect. That bottle was my only physical evidence at the time and it was lost. I did not follow up with my team to be sure that all the i's were dotted and t's were crossed. Even if we had not gotten the finger print, if we had that bottle, with today's technology, we may be able to get DNA evidence to try to match in CODIS. With a match, we would have the killer." With a look a regret, he paused then continued, "You've done a great job gettin' up to speed, Mason. You found the Achilles heel in such a short period of time. Reckon, I knew you would. You never talked about working a cold case. But, thought you might be a good fit for this one, since you live on Folly. People over there don't tend to trust law officers. You don't look too intimidatin'. And you're smart as a whip. Thought you might have some local connections. You've met the qualifications to be promoted temporarily to the cold case unit. However, you have one case and you report directly to me. Now go solve Megan Taylor's Cold Case." Palmer stared into her eyes as if he expected her to jump out of the chair and run out of the room.

How in the world could this be happening? Something I've waited for my entire career. Yet now I feel frozen in fear to take the next step.

"So now I have the second piece of the favor. As you heard, I'm going on medical leave. I'm gonna ask you to take the lead investigator temporarily while I'm gone. You up to it?"

"Me? Why not Benedict? He has much more experience than me. He's been here a long time and generations of his family have been officers."

"It takes more than years of experience, time on the job, and family members to solve a mystery and to coordinate staff. You've shown me that you have the ability for deductive reasoning required to solve homicides. I want you to be the lead investigator during my temporary absence medical leave. I expect to be laid out at home for the next six weeks. You can call me and keep in the loop. Are you up for it, Officer Mason?"

"Yes, Sir."

14 VICTORIA'S INTERVIEW

"Interview Victoria Bennett
Charleston County Coroner's Office
8:47am May 1999"

Brooke inserted the tape and pressed play.
Immediately, she was struck by Victoria Bennett's attire.
*She looks more like a runway model than a Folly Beach resident
and College of Charleston student. I don't care if it's 1999 or
2023; She may have LIVED on Folly Beach...But she is not
FROM Folly Beach.* Brooke, familiar with Folly residents,
was not expecting Victoria to be dressed like she just
stepped out of a Nordstrom's Ad. Her ensemble
included a white button-down collared shirt, navy
double-breasted jacket, black nylon pants with pointy
pumps and a leather Louis Vuitton handbag large
enough to be a weekender.

"Good morning, Victoria Bennett, my name is
Detective Palmer and this is Detective Wainwright.
Your father mentioned that you knew Megan well. We
are hopeful that you may be able to help with our
investigation."

"Wait, I didn't know that you would be
recording this. Do you mind if I switch sides? My left
side is my better side." Victoria stood up and moved
her chair beside Detective Wainwright to place her left
side toward the video camera then began, "Meg was my
best friend. Dad told me that you found her on the
beach this morning." Victoria Bennett was holding a

tissue wiping her eyes as she spoke, "I can't believe that she's gone after knowing her all this time." Victoria paused as if she was having a difficult time getting her thoughts together. "We met on the very first day of graduate school and we've been best friends ever since."

"How long ago?"

"A little over two years ago."

"How did you meet?"

"My father had met her earlier when she interviewed for the Bennett Foundation Scholarship. Father had given me the full details of how both of Megan's parents are incarcerated for manufacturing and distribution of crack."

"Oh really? What do you know about Megan's parents?"

"Nothing, really. I do know that she was not close to them. She never mentioned them to me. Almost like she was trying to forget that she was born poor. Like using bleach, she just washed away her past, you know?"

"So, the two of you were close. What did the two of you have in common?"

"More than you would think. Lots of things. However, we were also very different." Victoria Bennett looked up to the two detectives sitting across from her, calmly she began to share her wisdom:

"When she interviewed for the scholarship. My father had explained to me that sometimes people are born with all of the ingredients to achieve greatness. However, they add zero effort and achieve the same." Victoria looked to her father for encouragement then continued. "Others are born with nothing, however with inspiration, work, time and effort they achieve greatness." Her father gave her a nod of encouragement.

"After Megan was awarded the scholarship, my dad had asked me to keep an eye on her. You know, make sure that she was successful in the master's program. I remember, we met on the first day and we've been together every single day for the last 2 years. She's our class valedictorian and I'm second. Some people think that second place is the same as the first loser. That's simply not true. Right, daddy?" Victoria began to cover her face with tissue to wipe away tears.

Palmer was patient for several seconds, then as she calmed herself, he took the opportunity to ask:

"Do you know of anyone who would want to hurt Megan?"

"Do you imagine that someone did this to Megan on purpose?!" Victoria began to look upset; a look of surprise and anguish at the same time. Then asked:

"You don't think that she drowned?"

"Do you?" Palmer asked.

"How do I know? You are the expert."

"Can you think of anyone else that was close to Megan?"

"She and Dr. Bob Bathe, her advisor at CoC were close. They spent hours together outside of class in the lab doing research."

"Can you think of anyone who had a problem with Megan?"

"Maybe one of those surfing men; She's always spending time with them." Victoria paused for several seconds, then looked toward her father.

"Oh Daddy, do I have to continue to think about these things? It's just so stressful to me." She began to cover her eyes with her tissue and cry.

Her father, Dr. Bennett, began to console her. "No, you don't have to sit here any longer, Tori. You've answered all the questions. I'm sure you've been a big help to the investigation." He turned towards the camera:

"As you can imagine, Detective Palmer, it has been a very difficult day for Tori and me. If you'll excuse us, we're no longer able to answer your questions."

Dr. Bennett reached for Victoria's hand and helped her from the seat as he placed his arm around her shoulder to comfort her. She began to sob louder and threw her arms around her father and together they cried.

Palmer walked to the door, opened it, and said,

"Absolutely. You've been a huge help. We appreciate your time. If you think of anything else that would be beneficial to our case, please reach out." The video ended.

Brooke added the professor's name to her growing list of people that she wanted to find and interview:

Ryan Willis

Dr. Raymond Bennett

Dr. Bob Bathe

Yeah, thinkin' because he's a professor at The College of Charleston, he will have an electronic trail as well. Hopefully just an internet search for him.

15 AUTOPSY

Brooke decided to find the autopsy report next. She opened the lid and was amazed at how many pieces of paper had been crammed into the file box. Unable to flip through the tightly packed documents, Brooke removed a large stack. Beginning to sort through the now freed papers and file folders, she located the manilla folder with "AUTOPSY" handwritten in black thick permanent marker and a laser printed label:

Legal Name: Taylor, Megan Rose
Date of Birth: 03/31/1975
Date of Death: 05/16/1999

Can't believe that Megan was only a few years younger than me when she was murdered. She was just getting ready to launch into the world.

Brooke opened the folder and started to read the first page of the MUSC pathologist's transcripts, "This 24-year-old female was found to be unresponsive in the ocean surf of Folly Beach at Washout this morning. *Just three years younger than me.* She was pronounced dead at the scene by Coroner Burgess at 06:47 am. Positive identification was provided by her driver's license and verified by her employer Dr. Raymond Bennett at the morgue prior to autopsy."

So, Dr. Bennett and Victoria went to the morgue to identify Megan and reported the relationship as employer.

General Appearance: Caucasian female of medium build, appears physically fit and well nourished, with defined musculature. *I bet that she was in good physical shape from all that swimming and surfing. Wonder if I would have liked her?*

Height: 5'8"

Weight: 132 pounds

Skin: Pruning noted on hands and feet from extended exposure to water pre and post mortem. *So, she was in the water before and after she was murdered causing her skin to shrivel up.* Two rows of ligature marks noted on her neck ⅝" each. *The rope or cord left marks as it was wrapped around her neck twice.* Also of note are three scratch marks on skin of the posterior region of her neck. *Wonder if those scratches on the back of her neck were made by Megan or her killer? It sounds like Megan was choked to death with a cord. Probably her surfboard leash.* Also, upon further inspection, of note are her displaced metacarpal joints with edema and ecchymosis present. *She had broken knuckles with swelling and bruising.* Her fingernails have jagged tips. *The swelling, bruising and jagged fingernails indicate that she fought her attacker. Definitely defensive wounds.*

Tattoo: Lumbosacral region. See attached photos for description. Brooke glanced at the attached photo. *The usual tramp stamp tattoo on the low back.*

Birthmark: Left lower extremity 3.5 inches distal to inferior patella measuring ¾" circular. *Discolored skin on her left lower leg just below her knee cap.*

Scar: Right eye brow measured at ½"; Left forearm lower ⅓ measures 2 ½".

Abrasions present over bilateral knees and shins. *Scrapes on both of her knees and shins. Further confirmation of my theory about our victim being forced down the beach. Looks like fresh sand burns on her legs.*

Musculo-skeletal Exam: Acute edema noted over posterior thoracic spine. Swelling on her back between the shoulder blades. That's an odd place to have swelling.

Hyoid fracture. *Bone in the front of her neck is broken.*

Eyes: petechial hemorrhage noted. *The blood vessels in Megan's eyes broke when she was being choked. That happens with a rope type choking, called ligature asphyxiation. I wonder if the Medical Examiner collected nail clippings? Wait… If there are nail clippings, there could be DNA evidence. Science has significantly improved since 1999. If the nail clippings were saved by the medical examiner, then maybe we can use them for DNA testing. That may be the answer to the missing Mountain Dew bottle.*

16 CALIFORNIA DREAMING

Brooke was lost in thought as she drove to California Dreaming. *Maybe I'll go with the steak. Oh! But I love the she-crab soup! Or shrimp tacos and their salad. Definitely gotta have the salad. Best house dressing known to humans. I don't even like that type of dressing... But I've been known to lick the bowl. Or sop it up with the fresh out of the oven croissant delicately brushed with honey. I don't like honey either!!! Something about the way that the warm croissant and the cold salad with warm dressing come together. Definitely a splurge!!*

Mouth watering about her food choices, she turned left into the Ripley Light Marina entrance. As she drove along the water's edge, the private yachts lined the edge of the marina. She always enjoyed people watching at the water's edge. It was filled with eclectic people with a variety of goals. Some visitors came with plans of drinking while touring the Charleston Coastline aboard a private party boat. Other visitors to the marina come to experience a private nature tour for the day. Still others, Brooke's favorite, came to charter a fishing yacht. She amused herself by reading the names printed on the transoms of the sport fishing yachts. The captain's controls, located high above the boat deck, were designed to give the captain an advantage in spotting large schools of fish in the water. Each day after fishing, the sunburned fisherman would exit the boat onto the docks after being on "sea legs" all day. They often walked like drunken sailors to the shore with larger-than-life stories about their bucket list day.   It was Brooke, Corley and Joleen's habit to meet on the docks to walk along, reading the names and creating stories about owners.

First to arrive, Brooke read the first name, "Storm Teaser". *Maybe a meteorologist? Or a hair stylist? How about a meteorologist with big 80s hair?!* Laughing out loud, she was startled when Corley appeared behind her.

"Starting without us, are you?"

Relieved to see her friend smiling, "Just couldn't help myself. Your turn."

Corley looked to the next transom for a name. A sleek yacht with beautiful lines, it read, "A Reel Lady".

Corley began.

"A plastic surgeon… Or a mannequin manufacturer!"

"That's a good one... Corley, how do you do it? Joleen's turn…"

She read the next yacht transom, "Mega-bytes."

"Okay, so I do get the tech reference. But it's not that funny, brainier. How about the creator of the movie *Megamind* eaten one mouthful at a time?" They all laughed.

"We never said that they have to make sense!" Joleen defended her turn at the game.

"Okay, Brooke! I challenge you. Yours is even harder!"

Brooke began. "Lady Jane, the mother of a sarcastic daughter named Joleen!"

Again, they laughed until Joleen demanded that they stop because she had her "giggle box" turned over and her face was starting to hurt."

74

Trying not to laugh, they quietly walked the short distance to California Dreaming Restaurant. Once inside, Joleen made her way to the ladies' room while Brooke and Corley waited in the six-sided tower at the top of the staircase entrance. Corley opened the door for a family of four: the mother with the sleeping child in her arms, and for the father with the six-ish looking boy who was hesitant to enter.

"Is it a real castle?"

"It's built to look like a castle, but it's not old. It's kinda like a new castle."

"Then where are the knights?"

The curious boy questioned his father. He and now Brooke looked to the exasperated father and waited for the answer. It was the matrade that interrupted Brooke's lock on his face. Without hearing the father's answer, the three co-workers followed the hostess past the turret looking entrance. Immediately, the vastness of the open space became apparent. As Brooke noticed the bar to the left, she gawked at the large variety of potions available with and without spirits. *The beauty of the raised bar is worth the visit alone.* Beyond the elevated bar, the several story tall windows overlooked the Ashley River, making every seat in the place perfect for looking over the water and the marina. Once seated, she noticed the Hatteras yacht entering from the rough waters of the inlet.

"Isn't that just beautiful?" as she motioned towards the yacht.

"It's really the thought of sailing away that's beautiful." It was Corley. "Something about being on

75

the water… feels like a vacation every time."

"Change Order" was artfully written across the transom of the 59-foot private vessel. It sailed steadily through the inlet with dolphins swimming through the spray at the stern of the vessel.

"Change Order… I don't get it." Joleen wrinkled her brow.

As the grand boat passed by, Brooke noticed the 19' dinghy raised above the deck. Moving further inland, she could read the dinghy name "original contract." She giggled through her explanation that the original contract allowed the owner to purchase the 19' dinghy and the change orders allowed for the purchase of the yacht. They laughed together at the names then began to quietly look at the menus.

Corley spoke first. "I'm going all in today. I'm having the Shrimp and Grits… love that andouille Sausage and the real South Carolina Adluh grits. What are y'all having?"

"Definitely gonna have the California Dreaming Salad! It's my favorite…and having comfort food today. Lovin' the Baked Potato Soup!"

"Joleen, how about you? What are you having?"

"I love the baby back ribs, but that's just too much food… I'm gonna have the Charleston Seafood pasta."

"Now that we got the pleasantries and food orders out of the way, give us the scoop on your cold case."

"Joleen, I'm gonna need some help on this cold case."

"You sound like a detective. All work and no play already?" It was Corley, trying unsuccessfully to talk about something other than work.

"Anything I can do to help. What do you need?"

"Find Ryan Willis. He's the 911 caller from the cold case that I'm working."

"No problem, just forward everything you have gathered about him: full name, last employer, driver license number, and if you have a social, all the better!"

"Well, that's the problem. I know nothing. Except that 23 years ago he was a surfer on Folly that called 911 to report Megan Taylor's death."

"That's it? Damn it Brooke, I'm an officer of the law, not a magician." Joleen stared through her glasses into Brooke's eyes without blinking. Joleen's twangy southern drawl was as sweet as honey. However, at times her cornflower blue eyes were piercing as if she could teleport her thoughts directly into Brooke's mind like Spock. *Wonder if Spock ever sent curse words?! Message received!* Not wanting to mind-meld any longer, she responded.

"As I gather more information, I will pass it on to you. Just hoping that you will work your magic."

"There's definitely a limit to my abilities. Is there anything else?"

"Yeah, Find Dr. Raymond Bennett, Dr. Bob Bathe and set up interviews. Do you know if the Medical Examiner's office keeps nail clippings?"

17 MORNING GET AWAY

Brooke could no longer sleep and tapped her phone for the time. *5:17 am. An hour until sunrise, plenty of time for my morning ritual of sunrise jog on the beach.* She moved quickly and silently to gather things that she would need for today: purple Juicy Couture backpack, Ford Escape keys, Yeti cup filled with water, gym bag, and her dark blue Charleston County Police Department Uniform. Quietly, she exited the efficiency apartment where she lived under the multi-million-dollar beautiful beach home. Now outside and continuing to work in total darkness under the stilted home, she loaded the Ford Escape with her things. Then she stepped into the relative privacy of the outdoor shower with her gym bag. She used the spicket water to brush her teeth and changed into her long black yoga pants, her Aerie support athletic bra, and her lightweight New Balance running shoes, no socks. "Socks and beach just don't mix", Brooke had once told her boyfriend, Jacob. Although the expected high temperature was 80 degrees today, fairly normal for mid-May in South Carolina, the windy predawn drive along the beach at washout would be a little chilly for a tank top alone. Hanging on the hook inside the outdoor shower, she found and adorned her favorite Ocean Surf Shop hoodie.

Wanting to get away from the apartment before Jacob realized that she had gotten out of bed, Brooke

drove down the gravel driveway away from her
efficiency apartment. Glad to escape the unspoken
stress of a relationship that she had already outgrown.
Jacob and Brooke had been dating over the last several
months. Like a seagull to a beach goers picnic lunch,
she had a knack for attracting those who had "fallen
down" and just needed a little help to get back on their
feet. Her mother had called them "broken sparrows".
Brooke could hear her mother's voice:

"Jacob sounds like another "broken sparrow" to
me. You really know how to pick 'em Brookey."

*I'm willing to admit to myself that I try to see the good in
people, sometimes to my own detriment. And I admit that I have
a knack for choosing to get involved with men who "have lots of
potential for self-development". But Jacob is a good guy, we have
fun. Maybe I just haven't found the right one. In the meantime,
Jacob is... comfortable. And I love his dog!*

Once she reached the end of the driveway and
turned left onto E Ashley Avenue, Brooke began her
morning ritual prayer.

*Lord, be with me today. Help me to do your will. Help
me to let go of worry about things over which I have no control.
Let go of all thoughts that are non-productive. Amen.*

Brooke began to clear her mind as she drove
along the narrow street with the ocean to her right and
huge hundred-year-old live oak trees to her left. The
live oaks provided shade from the moonlight; her path
was only luminated by the headlights of her Ford
Escape. Soon the trees gave way to marshy grass.
Finally, arriving at washout, Brooke stepped out of her
crossover to smell the salty ocean breeze.

I must be one of the luckiest people on earth!

The coastal wind now blowing through her frizzy hair, she took a moment to feel the freedom before pulling it into a low bun with a scrunchie, then resumed her self-talk:

I love feeling like I am part of nature. At one with the wind while alone on my morning jog. At one with the sand dunes to my right. At one with the rocky jetties on my left. And at one with an endless beach.

Brooke's mind began to wonder as she jogged the six miles of beach along Folly. The island was named so in 1696 for the thick brush and undergrowth along the coast of the island. Later, it was called Coffin Island. Not for the burial box, but for the last name of plantation owners in Beaufort and Charleston. Today, the seven square mile beach is perfect for vacationers wanting to surf, sunbath, and enjoy the Atlantic shore. Although humans are welcome to share the beach, many interesting creatures make their home on Folly. It's the turtles and pelicans that have used the island for generations. As Brooke jogged along, she noticed a sandcastle and hole in the beach. She stopped her jog to cover the hole. Using her feet, Brooke covered the hole as she remembered the words of Sea Turtle Foundation Community Leader, Murphy Wainwright during the most recent beach sweep.

They impede mother turtles from making their way up to the dunes where they lay eggs. In the later months when the babies hatch, holes and sandcastles impede the babies from making it to the safety of the ocean before they get gobbled up by birds. Having leveled the sandcastle and the adjoining hole, she resumed her jog. Her mind began to wonder how the turtle populations were doing.

Although Brooke Mason rented an apartment on Folly Beach, she spent most of her days on the contrasting Kiawah Island (also a sea turtle sanctuary) where she was a member of the MAIT for the Charleston County Police Department. Unlike the local vibe of Folly Beach, Kiawah Island attracted a more international traveler. The Island Luxury Resort has hosted multiple professional golf tournaments at the Ocean Course. As the crow flies, the two beaches were only nine miles apart, however they were widely separated by the Stono River inlet and socioeconomic status. To commute from Folly Beach to Kiawah Island each day for work, Brooke drove the 29 miles around the Stono river inlet. It would take her between 52 and 65 minutes to cross the bridge at Bohicket Road Highway 700, then back towards the coast.

18 BROOKE'S IMPROVEMENT

Brooke crossed the street and glanced at her phone which showed 5:29 am. *Perfect, sunrise is 6:13 and high tide was at 5:11 AM.* Always aware of her surroundings, she noted a lone car parallel parked along E Ashley Avenue on the beach side of the public parking area. Between the car and the sand dune was a very tan, blond-haired middle-aged guy wearing a wetsuit. While removing his surfboard from the racks on top of the older car, he briefly looked up and gave a nod to Brooke as she jogged past him, as if acknowledging her for being out on the beach at this time of the morning.

Yeah, only the dedicated are out here before first light.

Brooke began to reflect on her time spent on Folly Beach as a child while learning to surf. Surfing takes commitment and dedication to being on your board whenever the tide calls. She had developed these qualities from a young age. Growing up in a very poor household, she had become determined to be financially self-sufficient. She believed that with hard work, she could accomplish any goal... if she was willing to put in work, time, and her best effort. Keywords: work, time, and best effort. Just like with many other activities in life, she had observed numerous people have dreams of accomplishing things yet, never act on the ideas OR

choose goals that made no sense. She had observed
other people attempt new activities like surfing: sinking
hundreds or thousands of dollars into custom boards,
lessons, and clothing only to inhale a little ocean water
on the first few attempts and give up on the surfing
dream.

*Yes. Commitment and Dedication were very important
qualities. But realistic goal setting is the key to success.*

Just as Brooke stepped down from the
boardwalk over the dune at Washout and onto the
beach, her phone pinged to indicate a voicemail. It was
a message from Sergeant Palmer. Her patrol shift didn't
start until 07:00 am, so Brooke continued her sunrise
morning jog. She loved being one of the only bipedal
creatures on the beach at this time of the morning. She
felt that she was getting away with something by being
fortunate enough to see the sun rise over the Atlantic
Ocean nearly every day. She reminded herself that
Megan no longer has the same fortune. Her life had
been cut short at about this time of the morning. *If she
and I were alive at the same time, I wonder if I would see her on
the beach at this crazy time of the morning.* In deep thought,
she began to jog along the dune side of tide pools on
the dry firmly packed beach.

Still jogging several minutes later as the sun
started to reflect on the glassy surface of the sand, she
began to give herself affirmations. *Proud of myself for the
internal drive to prove— I mean, to <u>improve</u> myself each day. Was
that a Freudian slip? That's a big difference, isn't it? The
difference between "proving" myself and "improving" myself. A
big difference, the tiny little "im" that my brain had left out of my*

thought process. The word "prove" insinuates trying to convince others. A much more menacing, unhealthy thought process. In contrast im-proving myself was just trying to be one smidgen better at anything than the day before. A much better thought process. Okay, so convince yourself. Yell it to the world.

"I'm improving myself today! Don't forget the "I-M". Brooke called out to the empty beach.

Feeling confident after yelling at the beach, she entered the boardwalk over the dunes. Remembering the vital role that dunes play in maintaining the shore, she was careful not to damage any of the seagrass. The plants' roots hold the sand dunes, humanity's only defense against mother nature's wrath during the high tide each day. Now back at her car, her thoughts returned to the voicemail from Palmer and started to wonder why he would call her so early again this morning.

"If he would just learn to text!" Brooke muttered.

Upon returning to her Ford Escape, Brooke climbed in, locked the door, and opened her device to listen to the voicemail.

"Mason, this is Palmer. Report straight to headquarters."

Immediately Brooke felt physically sick with anticipation. All of the prayer, self-talk, and exercise to calm her generalized anxiety now out the window. Brooke felt like she was going to throw up.

19 MURPHY WAINWRIGHT

Upon entering headquarters, Officer Brooke Mason stopped at Joleen's desk. The top of which was perfectly organized and almost void of paper. Joleen did not keep sticky notes on her desk. It was a purposeful move. Long ago she told Brooke in her sweet southern voice. "I had to make a rule about people puttin' yeller notes on my desk. I'd walk away for a blip of a second and come back to a desk covered in so many yeller sticky notes, it looked like Big Bird trying to take flight. All those things flappin' at me. Had to make a rule... No yeller Notes!" She placed the latte in the center with a scribbled note on the cup: "Thank you for being Joleen!" Disappointed that Joleen had not been there to greet her, Brooke continued on to her makeshift office in the small interrogation room.

Now in the quiet of her own workspace, Brooke began to retrieve message after message from Joleen. "Murphy Wainwright, founder of Sea Turtle Conservation Foundation, is here. When he came into HQ this morning, he told me that he had a meeting with Palmer." "Palmer asked that you report directly to his office upon arrival at HQ." Before Brooke could make a move, Joleen's voice encouraged her to stand quickly. "Looks like Officer Brooke Mason is around here somewhere, let me fetch her to your office." Her voice was getting louder as she neared the open door. Within seconds, Joleen was standing in the doorway motioning for Brooke to follow her. As she followed, Brooke could hear Joleen whisper: "Did you get my messages?"

Keeping in step with Joleen's much longer legs, Brooke whispered back: "Yes, this very second."

Joleen and Brooke entered Palmer's office, who was sitting at his desk with his forward baseball catcher posture, intently listening to the older man sitting across from him in the "hot seat". Only, it didn't appear to be so much of a "hot seat" today. The man immediately rose and held his hand out to shake Brooke's as he introduced himself. "You must be Lead Detective Brooke Mason. Pleased to meet you. I'm Murphy Wainwright."

"As in the founder of the Sea Turtle Conservation Foundation?
"Yes, One and the Same! As a matter of fact, Palmer was just telling me that you are a resident of Folly? Where? Thought that I knew most of the locals. Been livin' there all my life."

As if by instinct, he held up his hand to give the Folly wave. Brooke returned the wave with her thumb, and pinky fingers extended as she sat in the seat beside Mr. Wainwright. Using the same strategy as last time she was in the hot seat, she remained quiet. However, unlike last time, she maintained her confident posture and squared her shoulders towards the visitor. His face looked so familiar. Yet Brooke just couldn't place it. The long schnauzer of a nose was really familiar along with the wild hair, that face.

I've seen him somewhere recently... besides being the Sea Turtle guy. But before she could place the face, Palmer began to speak.

"Officer Byrd, would you please close the door behind you?" He obviously wanted a private conversation and Joleen was not to be included. As Joleen passed Brooke, she winked then closed the door. Now, with the three alone, Palmer leaned forward, folding his forearms on the desk. His voice was quiet yet firm and deliberate. "Murphy and I go way back. He and I worked together on Megan's case before he left law enforcement to go start the foundation. He's been my informant on Folly for over 20 years. I've told him you are taking lead on Megan Taylor's case and that I have full confidence in you. That you are an outstanding officer who lives on Folly. However, to keep you safe, he has agreed to be your informant as well. Says that he knows that Megan Taylor was considering making a formal complaint against Dr. Bob Bathe at the time of her death."

"Really, what is your source? How do you know this?" Brooke knew that she was being pushy.

"Well, if I give MY source, I won't be trusted by the locals. I will just say that there are many things to be learned at the local table at Locklear's. I go for the shrimp and grits, but stay for the scoop. If you are not a local, it's "No scoop for you!" He laughed at himself and Palmer joined in. Brooke didn't get what was so funny about "no scoop for you". She waited again for one of them to speak.

"A reliable source has reason to believe that Megan Taylor's advisor, Dr. Bob Bathe, may be involved in her demise."

"That sounds so vague." The words had

escaped Brooke's mouth before she realized that it sounded unappreciative of the lead. "I mean, do you have any details about how he was involved or what his motive would be?"

"Hey. As an informant, I don't ask questions, I just listen. Then inform Palmer of anything that I hear."

"Well, what did you hear?"

"That the murderer must be that professor, Dr Bob Bathe or the surfer that found her. I happen to know Ryan Willis. It was NOT him.

"How can you be so sure that it was NOT him?"

"He's a good guy. Shows up to all of the beach clean ups. Hasn't gotten into any more trouble."

"How do you know?"

"Cause he's a LOCAL!"

Brooke was not convinced, but she dropped the line of questioning when she noticed the stern look on Palmer's face. It was apparent that he didn't approve of her questioning a long-time informant of his. She was expected to be gracious for the informant and the lead. Palmer took control of the conversation.

"Officer Mason, you and Corley have an interview with Dr. Bob Bathe this morning. He has been cooperative and agreed to answer questions in his home. If in the line of questions, there is probable cause, complete the paperwork immediately. We want to nip this in the bud. We will get that warrant within minutes. Now go. Corely is waiting in the parking lot and Dr. Bob Bathe is expecting you."

20 DR. BOB BATHE

As they entered the live oak lined driveway, Brooke mentally prepared herself for the interview. She took a deep breath and blew it out as slowly as possible.

My goal is to gather new information. I need to establish rapport with the professor (and Maryanne here on Gilligan's Island.) Her brain triggered from all those years of watching Sherwood Schultz sitcoms.

Focus Brooke. Ok. The interview with Dr. Bob Bathe. Then she whispered to Detective Corley:

"Remember the Dr. conversation guidelines; Whether it's an MD, PHD, or DO, most expect to be called 'doctor'. They are well-educated, effective communicators who are great at debate... Allow them to talk. Ask open-ended questions. Do not corner them or they will escape."

Because they are the same height, Brooke could see and hear the smile in his voice as Corley whispered back. "You've been talking to Palmer so much! You're starting to think like him. He does the same thing... Talks to himself, then whispers a plan on how to perform the most effective interview." Comparing her to Palmer was a huge compliment. Although it may not sound like a compliment at the moment, it did help to calm her. Brooke was nervous to enter her first official cold case interview; she wanted to exude confidence. She knew the importance of posture and poise when gathering information. Just before Corley rang the bell, she reminded herself to maintain a relaxed posture and open body language to help a witness to feel comfortable while sharing information. She started to remind Corley about body posture however, she thought better of it and remained quiet instead.

Once inside the office, she noticed the dank smell of damp paper. Three of the walls were dominated by adjustable shelving and were filled floor to ceiling with black magazine holders. Although the built-in cabinetry had been white when new, it was now dingy with age. The black holders were filled with professional periodicals and journals.

Charleston humidity and lots of absorbent paper, no wonder it smells moldy in here.

The two windows behind Dr Bob Bathe's desk provided some relief from the extremely mundane walls of his office. This time of the day, the morning sun illuminated the dark silhouette of the man behind the desk, making it difficult to read the expression on his face. Sitting in his black swivel chair behind his neatly organized desk, his outline looked nefarious against the bright window behind him.

"Dr. Bob Bathe, thank you for meeting with us on such short notice. I'm Detective Mason and this is my college Detective Corley with the Charleston County Police Department."

"When you mentioned Megan Taylor on the phone, I was intrigued to hear that someone is working on her case after all this time." Without getting up, he gestured with his hand, inviting them to sit in the two chairs across from his desk. Once seated, Brooke began her fact-finding mission with open-ended questions:

"So, tell me, what do you remember about Megan Taylor?"

"It's been 23 years. However, I did read my notes to re-familiarize myself. What do you want to know?" Shrugging his shoulders, Dr. Bathe folded his arms on the desk.

Signs of separating himself. Is he feeling threatened already? Brooke leaned back in her chair and placed each forearm on the armrest to be less threatening and asked another open question.

"How well did you get to know each other?"

"Megan Taylor was a graduate student. I was an advisor and lab supervisor. We conducted research together." Still leaning forward, he brought his hands together, then to his mouth.

Is he trying to remind himself to keep his mouth shut… to not say any more than is required to answer the question? Is that why he covered his mouth? Brooke wanted him to speak more freely. She continued to ask open-ended questions.

"Tell us about Megan's academic career."

"As a graduate student, she excelled in academia and research, here at the College of Charleston. She applied herself and was the recipient of the Bennett Foundation Scholarship. This is a very prestigious scholarship as the recipient is expected to perform cutting edge research worthy of publication prior to graduation. Megan Taylor had earned a master's degree in exercise physiology in 1999 when she… What specifically is it that you want to know?"

"Do you remember anything suspicious just before Megan's murder?"

"I will never forget, 1999 was the year of "Columbine". Everyone on every campus was suspicious. You're too young to remember the Columbine Massacre. But you do know about it, right?" He stopped and looked to Brooke to acknowledge his question.

Brooke knew that agreement would help to develop rapport.

"Yeah, you're right, I'm too young to remember the Columbine Massacre. And you're right again. I do know about the 13 innocent lives that were lost that day. Campus security was forever changed." Brooke asked a more direct question:

"Do you know anyone who may have wanted to harm Megan?"

"No. She was liked by her classmates."

"Speaking of classmates, were there any that stood out to you as friends, lovers?"

Dr. Bathe crossed his arms and leaned back in his chair. He stopped making eye contact and closed his eyes as if trying to recall a long-lost memory.

"I recall that she and Dr Bennett's daughter," He raised his hand to his head, continuing to think.

"What's her name?"

"Victoria, That's it. She and Victoria Bennett were close friends. As far as a lover, not anyone that I know, but I do know that she and Victoria were inseparable except when Megan was surfing. Have you talked to Victoria Bennett? And her sidekick Ken— I mean, Guy Andrews? As I recall, it was Megan that had given Guy the Nickname Ken. You know, like Ken and Barbie. The three of them were always together. It's hard to believe that she could die doing what she loved so much."

Brooke moved her head to make eye contact with the professor before she asked another question. She wanted to see the reaction in his eyes.

"Was there anyone who may want to harm Megan Taylor?"

Pausing again, He closed his eyes and brought his hand to his imaginary "data recall button" in the center of his forehead before he spoke.

"I was always suspicious of the way Guy looked at Megan. He could not keep his eyes off of her. He was so protective of her. Have you seen how muscular he is? Just made me wonder…"

Patiently, Brooke again waited for Dr. Bathe to look up from his "thinking posture" to make eye contact before she asked

"Did you know Megan Taylor personally as well?"

Looking into Brooke's eyes and then into Corely's eyes, he protested.

"I was her advisor and mentor." Putting his hands over his mouth again, he stopped.

After a short silence, Corely was much more direct.

"Did she ever mention that she was concerned about her safety, about Guy Andrews or anyone else?" Both detectives looked squarely at Dr. Bathe waiting for a direct answer.

"No. She never did appear to ever be concerned for her own safety. She was pretty good at taking care of herself. However, she spent most mornings muttering about some fellow surfer."

"How about a name?" Corely questioned, then quickly looked down to his device to document the conversation as if waiting for an exact spelling.

The "data recall button" was utilized once again. Apparently to no avail this time, as the Dr. was unable to retrieve the information.

"No. Don't think she ever mentioned a name. Just that he was there every morning… used to make her angry some mornings. Stealing her set. And celebrating other mornings."

"How about you, Dr Bob Bathe? Did you have a personal relationship? Did you make her angry? Or better yet, did she make you angry?"

"We spent countless hours together journaling research, analyzing the data, writing the dissertation, and preparing to defend it. Absolutely we disagreed. We had a difference in our professional opinions." He crossed his hands as if the statement relieved him of any fault for previous wrongdoings.

Brooke, on the other hand, heard one word. She repeated:

"Journals… What type of journals?"

Suddenly, Dr Bathe looked up towards Brooke and Corley. The distress at the mere mention of the word "journal" had created an apparent fear reaction in the professor. He took a millisecond to regroup his emotions. Keeping them in check, he answered,

"Research. You wouldn't understand, it's all biological and medical documentation."

"May I see them, please?" Brooke didn't fall for the bait of his remark and remained silent. After several long seconds of a stare-off, Dr. Bob Bathe stood up with a huff, looking annoyed, and shuffled to the shelving opposite corner of the desk, pulled the black journal holder to the edge of the shelf, and removed the binder with the year 1999 printed on the back. He turned to place the binder on his desk when his wife could be heard walking down the short hallway.

Obviously, several decades younger than Dr. Bob Bathe, Janice entered the home office with a smile like a Quinceanera princess on her 15th birthday. However, instead of a teenager's gown, she was dressed like the Charleston, SC fashionista blogger Anabelle K. Barnett, ready for a photo shoot. She kissed his cheek as she entered the dark room, handed the professor his reading glasses, then turned to Brooke and Corley.

"I don't think that we have met. I'm Janice Bathe, Bob's wife."

"Hello, I'm Officer Brooke Mason and this is Officer Corley. Part of the Major Accident Investigation Team. We are here to ask a few questions about Megan Taylor."

"Yes, Bob was very upset all night after reading those journals to… what did you say, "re-familiarize" yourself with Megan Taylor. Didn't you say last night that she's the former student that drowned while surfing on Folly? Back in like, 1999?"

"So, you're not familiar with Megan Taylor?" Corely was looking to Janice Bathe to answer the question.

"Oh no! … I was only 12 in 1999, born in 1987. Graduated from high school in 2004." She smiled as if she was proud to be so many years his junior.

Wanting to keep her talking, Brooke turned her attention and asked Mrs. Bathe. "So how did you and Dr. Bathe meet?"

Janice Bathe's face lit up. She sat in the chair near Brooke and crossed her legs at the ankles.

"It's such a fun story. We were both at Spoleto and he happened to sit beside me at the event. We bantered small intellectual jokes back and forth before the performance... Then during the climax of the event, I caught him sniffing my hair. He said that he could not resist… So romantic! I was so flattered! After the show, we could both tell that we wanted more intellectual banter. Lucky for us, the performance had been at the CoC Sottile Theatre. We stayed for hours talking and laughing. That was 2010. It was only five years later that Bob retired, right? Can you believe that it's only been eight years since we married?! Time flies by. Can I bring you anything before I meet the girls at Spoleto?

"Spoleto?" Dr Bathe questioned with a furrowed brow.

Janice's face again lit up and her smile dominated her face. "Yes, remember, It's May 29. I'm going to Spoleto to see Ayodele Casel: Chasing Magic at 2 pm. She's the choreographer and tap dancer who is performing at the CoC Sottile Theatre."

As soon as his wife finished her sentence, Dr Bathe's face lit up like the Grinch who stole Christmas as he had the most brilliant excuse to end the interview. "Oh yes! I almost forgot about OUR plans for Spoleto today. I'm almost finished here with these officers." Now standing again, Dr. Bathe continued, "I'll be ready to escort you to the performance."

Brooke interjected: "To be honest with you, Dr Bathe, I have many more questions about your relationship with Megan Taylor. Also, I will need some time to review the journal entries you mentioned."

Anger filled Dr Bob Bathe's face. Nostrils flaring, large, black pupils nearly filling his gray-blue eyes: "Do you mean MY research journals?" The words were spoken through clenched teeth.

Not intimidated, Brooke faced the man as she spoke, "Do they include entries made by Megan Taylor around the time of her death?" Brooke wanted to be clear that he understood the relevance of the research journals.

"Yes, she was a graduate student. It was 1999! All the graduate students during that time made duplicate handwritten entries into the journals. Remember the big Y2K scare? I was not about to lose all of my data. I required that the graduate students document the data by handwritten entries in addition to entering it into the computer system." He nearly snarled like a wolf ready for attack.

Brooke leaned forward as she reminded Dr. Bathe. "I'm here as an officer of the law conducting an investigation. I'm asking for access to the journal entries

97

from January to May of 1999 made by Megan Taylor."

"I'm not going to be able to provide you with access to the journals today. As you are aware, I have prior commitments, and the journals contain proprietary information about my research."

"I will be glad to take the journals to HQ to perform MY research then bring them back to your home. That way we both get to enjoy our afternoon doing what we enjoy… you at the dance performance with your wife and me at HQ reviewing Megan's journal entries."

"Not going to happen, no way will I allow you to remove the professional journals or have access to them here, there, or anywhere. You'll need a search warrant to gain access to any of the journals." With that rant, Dr. Bathe pushed up from the seat and held his hand towards the office door. "Janice and I have plans." Sternly looking at Corley then Brooke, he escorted the detectives out of the office, down the long hallway, and out of the front door.

"Thank you for your time, Dr. Bathe." Was all that Brooke could muster as she thought she would explode from frustration.

21 SURVEILLANCE

Sitting in the unmarked Ford Escort parked across the street from the home of Janice and Dr. Bob Bathe, Brooke and Corley purposely decided to complete the interview documentation while keeping an eye on the professor.

"Let's make him a little nervous. Keep the car in the same spot. See if he goes to Spoleto."

"He's definitely hiding something…" Corley was making notes in his laptop about the Dr. Bathe interview while it was fresh on their minds.

"Yeah, why doesn't he want us to see the journals? Why didn't he just give us access?" Brooke definitely felt that something in those journals made the professor uneasy. "He must be hiding something. But what?"

"I'm not sure, but I'm sending a request to Officer Joleen Byrd as we speak to request a warrant. And for Dr. Bob Bathe to make a formal statement down at headquarters. Let's make him a little more uncomfortable." Corley always followed department procedures and processes. "I think that he knew Megan better than he is willing to admit."

"Yeah, he was definitely defensive, a sign of not being truthful. Otherwise, why would he have read through everything last night? Was he looking for something in particular?"

"That's a great point. Did he realize that

something in those research journals would incriminate him?"

"It is rather odd that the information was stored in his home. After all, he retired from CoC over eight years ago. Megan's journal entries would have happened over 23 years ago. But what does he have to hide?"

"Not sure. But something's off."

"What was the other name that he mentioned?" Corley referred to his laptop notes... Guy Andrews."

"I definitely want to talk to him. Ask Joleen to invite him to headquarters for an interview."

Corley types on the laptop for a few seconds then looks up to Brooke. "Did you see his wife, Janice? She must be..."

"36. She's 36 years old."

"And how old is Dr. Bob Bathe?"

"73. He's 73."

"Wow! Now that's a big generational gap. Wonder if he has always been attracted to women half his age?!"

22 GUY ANDREWS

As evidenced by his swollen eyes and red nostrils, Guy Andrews had been recently crying. He appeared very out of place and extremely anxious as he stood in front of the HQ double door entrance. His meek mannerisms were a contrast to his large, muscular body. According to the door frame yardstick, he was 6' 6" tall. Wearing a blue t-shirt and gray athletic shorts with running shoes, the outline of every muscle of his large frame were visibly defined.

He must spend every waking minute in the gym.

Although his body appeared to be perfectly maintained, his wavy hair was oily and disheveled in a million directions, as if he had not showered. He entered the police station then stood frozen in front of the massive doors, hands trembling, holding several spiral notebooks. His face had a look of conflict and dread, almost as if he was considering turning back to the door to escape the task at hand.

Brooke recognized him from his federal ID as Guy Andrews and didn't want to take the chance that he would reconsider. She began to make her way towards him. However, before she could speak, she heard Joleen's twangy southern drawl:

"Hey Mista And-drews. Thank you fir com'n down to the station. I'm Officer Byrd, we chatted on the phone yes'terday. You just don't know how much Officer Mason and I appreciate your time today."

"And I'm Officer Brooke Mason." Brooke couldn't believe that Joleen was first to the security check.

Before Brooke could speak again, Joleen took control in her strong southern drawl.
"Mista And-drews, won't you please come through the security check and follow me? We'll all have more privacy in one of our offices. Didn't you mention that privacy is extremely important to you?" Joleen remained facing the security check, but took two steps backwards and nodded towards Guy Andrews. Reluctantly at first, he placed the spiral notebooks into the checkpoint security bin. Then, placed his wallet and car keys in the separate small bin on the black conveyor. Finally, he stepped through the metal detector. The security officer waved him through then pointed to his notebooks, keys, and wallet as they exited the scanner.

"So glad that you are here." Joleen began before Brooke could speak.

"Welcome to headquarters, Mista And-drews." Joleen again walked to the security check down the hallway to the door of a small interview room. She opened the door and backed out of the room, holding her right arm to the side as if she were a game show host offering a curtain to a contestant.

As Guy Andrews walked into the small interview room, he pulled the notebooks close to his chest as if trying to protect them from any would-be thieves. Still holding the notebooks flat against his chest as if hugging himself, he sat in the chair. He looked down to the floor, not saying anything as Brooke and

Joleen entered the room. Once they were seated but before either officer began to question him, he looked down to the notebooks at his chest and whispered,

"These are her personal diaries."

Brooke, although excited about the revelation of the "potential diaries", began to speak calmly and slowly in an attempt to develop trust with the anxious man.

"As Officer Byrd mentioned on the phone, we are investigating the death of Megan Taylor and would like your help." Brooke could see tears forming in Guy Andrews' eyes and pondered the source of such a reaction to her name.

Why is he so upset, after 23 years? Does he know something about her death? Was he involved in some way? Did Guy Andrews murder Megan Taylor?

"Interview Guy Andrews on May 29 at 7:53 am Charleston County Headquarters. Officer Joleen Byrd and Brooke Mason present." With the formality out of the way, she leaned forward, attempting to make eye contact with Mr. Andrews. The one-foot height difference was apparent as Booke tilted her head backwards to look upward.

"For the record, please state your name, DOB, address and place of employment."

"Guy Beauregard Andrews, January 19, 1976, 115 W Oceanview Road, Charleston, SC 29412. Just You Fitness on James Island. I'm a personal trainer."

Now I know why he looks like a comic book advertisement. The bully on the beach image from the back cover. Well, much better looking... Focus!

"Mr. Andrews, thank you for volunteering to

meet with us today. We need your honesty and your help. Are you familiar with Megan Taylor?"

"Yes, we were very close."

"Tell me about the nature of your relationship."

Guy Andrews wiped his eyes with the back of his index knuckles and cleared his throat. He repositioned in his chair and began to tell his story. It sounded to Brooke like a well-rehearsed speech:

"Megan and I met on the first day of post graduate orientation at the University of Charleston, that's what we called the graduate school for CoC. You know, back in the late 90's when we were students there. I'll never forget that moment, it's etched into my memory forever. You see beforehand Tori's Dad, Dr. Bennett, had asked us to make Megan feel comfortable on her first day. It was apparent that he had some type of investment in her doing well. He had told us her backstory; about her parents being incarcerated and about the scholarship. To be honest, Tori and I were both dreading having to "babysit" some frail recluse all day. Boy, were we wrong about Megan. You see, back in 1999, we were in our early 20s. All the college girls wanted to look like one of the Spice Girls... Yeah, scary to me too." He looked over to Brooke and Joleen for the first time and began to shake his head side to side. Brooke and Joleen remained silent, encouraging him to continue. Without any prompting, he resumed his story.

"There she was... to be honest, I heard Megan Taylor's voice first. I'm from South Carolina, but her voice was so uniquely southern. It sounded like sweet molasses rolling off of her tongue. And I remember being drawn to it from across the lecture hall. But when I found the source; I was awestruck by her natural beauty. To this day… the most beautiful girl I've ever seen. Rarely wore make up. Didn't need it, either. Her skin was deep tan and had a body that you will never forget. She looked more like a Sports Illustrated swimsuit model than a graduate student. All the right curves in all the right places. When Victoria and I found Meg, she was engaged in conversation with several professors and outwardly appeared very confident on her first day. We waited until there was a lull in the conversation then introduced ourselves as fellow classmates. Megan turned around and spoke with the sweetest sounding voice. However, the words were a little sarcastic."

"You have got to be kid'n me! You two look like little ole Ken and Barbie! Bless y'all's sweet little hearts!"

Guy continued. "Instantly, I didn't like Megan. She and I were so different. Being raised in a traditional southern home, I had been taught to show grace by biting my tongue. She, on the other hand, asked all of the questions that others were afraid to ask. It was shocking and sometimes embarrassing initially, to have Meg say what was on her mind. That's one of the wonderful things about Megan… You never had to wonder what she was thinking. It was refreshing that she had no filter." Guy paused, took a deep breath, and dried his eyes with the back of his hand again.

"I really learned to appreciate her honesty."

"It sounds like Megan was one of a kind. Tell

me about your relationship in the days leading up to her homicide."

It was as if Guy Andrews had been waiting 23 years to tell the story. "Despite the fact that we had different backgrounds, we both loved anatomy, physiology and research. We both wanted to push the envelope of biomechanical performance. As we neared our time for internships, I couldn't tolerate the thought of being without Meg…"

Brooke interrupted: "Wait! Weren't you dating Victoria Bennett?"

"No, Victoria and I had stopped dating back in high school, we had continued to remain close friends."

"Friends with benefits?"

"Well, occasionally…" he sounded so matter of fact. Then he paused. As if caught, a look of surprise filled his face.

"No, really it wasn't like that…"

Joleen and Brooke remained silent as they both studied his facial expressions and body language change. He pushed back in his chair, crossed his tan muscular arms across his chest, and squinted his eyes a little as if trying to remember a well-rehearsed story from 23 years ago.

"Been Victoria's escort to many Charleston events since high school, for sure. But we had agreed long ago that we were not marriage material for each other."

"Are you trying to convince us that you and Victoria were no longer a couple?"

"Yes!"

"Mr. Andrews, it sounds like you believe it to be true. However, let me share the facts with you: One, you were high school sweethearts. Two, you attended public events together. Three, you spent most of each day together at CofC, and last but not least, you had a sexual relationship. The facts lead me to believe that you and Victoria meet my definition as dating... And you are trying to convince me that you were not a couple." Brooke noticed that Joleen had crossed her arms. Sitting next to Brooke, she could be intimidating when she used her cornflower blue eyes to stare without blinking. She also was waiting impatiently for him to respond.

"Really, we had talked about it many times after high school and throughout college. Nearing the end of college, I made a plan to move away. It was just some crazy coincidence that we were both accepted into the College of Charleston exercise science program together."

"Wait, That's a prestigious program. You expect us to believe that you both were accepted into the same graduate school, the same program in the same year?!" Brooke found it hard to believe his story. She knew that the acceptance rate for graduate schools was less than 5%. That's only about 9 positions for every 200 students who apply. Brooke questioned that Victoria Bennett and Guy Andrews were both top 5% student material.

"Well actually, I was the first alternate to the program. It was the craziest thing. Just the week before orientation, one of the students died in a tragic car accident."

"Ok, Wait. Before you continue. Just to be clear, if this student had not died in a car accident you would have attended a different graduate program?" Joleen was questioning this part of his statement.

"Yeah, I was all set to go to UNC Chapel Hill. Been assigned a roommate and everything. I had packed up to leave the next day. Victoria and I had said our goodbyes… The next morning, it was Dr. Bennett who called so early. He told me of the accident and that I was first alternate. I don't even remember applying to the College of Charleston graduate program. Dr Bennett and Victoria were both so happy that I made it into the program, I changed my plans and got an apartment here in Charleston. I guess I was meant to stay here. Destiny or something." Guy looked up as he was waking up from a time travel stupor, "I guess I wouldn't have met Megan, if Dr. Bennett hadn't convinced me to stay here all those years ago." With the end of his story, Guy pushed the spiral notebooks towards Brooke and stood up from the chair and began to walk to the door.

"Wait, I've got more questions."

"After you read Megan's diaries, call me. We can meet somewhere and talk. Preferably not here."

Brooke looked at diaries on the desk then back up at Guy, "Expect that call soon. We will process these as evidence. We appreciate your time today." Guy had already walked out of the room before she finished speaking.

23 MEGAN'S PERSONAL DIARY

May 12, 1999

Can't believe the day that I just had. Probably one of the best surfing days of my entire life! Spent the morning on the water! Wonderful sets at sunrise, toes were gripping the front of the board! Saw Ryan on the water.

Brooke wondered: *Is this the same Ryan that several days later made the 911 call?*

Gave me the Folly wave!

Brooke smiled. *That folly wave has been around as long as I can remember. It's the universal "I love you" made with the thumb, index and pinky fingers. She resumed reading:*

He had a good set! Good to not feel all alone in the water. Someone else as dedicated to surfing as I am! Love to start my day surfing.

Then had lunch with Tori. Always the drama queen!! She made a last-minute change with the photographer for the graduation party! Suddenly, she knows someone! Why didn't she come up with this sooner?! She waits until I find a photographer and hire them… WHATEVER! Guest list approved. Finally, I was able to confirm 148 people for the caterer. Band set. Graduation party coming together.

Brooke pondered: *Could this be the beach house manager duties that Dr. Bennett mentioned? Arranging for a graduation party for Victoria?* Brooke continued to read Megan's diary entry.

Tonight, I had a rehearsal session with Dr. Bob Bath to prepare for the "defense "of the research. There I was looking into the microscope at the newest form of fat eating microbe, when I

109

caught him smelling my hair! He just does not get my obvious hints! He is so brilliant, but really? Sniffing my hair. Freak.

Brooke thought: *A hair sniffer? Sounds familiar, but I just can't place where I've heard the reference before.*

When he asked me about my plans for later, I asked him how it was relevant to the research. NOT AT ALL! Hehehe.

Brooke began to be suspicious: *Dr Bob Bath had not divulged that he had been hitting on Megan Taylor.*

Luckily Guy came to the lab! Stopped that hair smelling really quick! Such a BIG help! Can't believe how close Guy and I have become... I surely misjudged him! Okay, the Nickname "Ken" was a little over the top. But my goodness! He looks like the live version of Ken! Except more muscular and more animated. We saw the movie There's Something about Mary. He uses references that crack me up!!! Asked Dr Bath if that was hair Gel on his lab jacket! He's Da Bomb!!

Brooke: *So far, it appears, Guy and Megan had a good relationship. Dr. Bath and Megan... Not so much!*

May 13, 1999

Feeling a little sickly this morning. Surfed anyway! Ryan was at the washout first! Can't believe he was so early. Acted like the self-appointed King of Folly. Broke in front of me many times. Stole my wave. Gonna get to Washout first and out paddle him tomorrow! Love/hate Ryan! Love to see him, but hate it when he shows off!

Tori's graduation party coming together. Here's the plan: May 16

1:00 pm. Graduation Day! Luckily, I can trust my friends at Lickety Pop Balloon Shop to oversee the set up while I graduate valedictorian. Lickety Pop Balloon Shop -

arrives at Bennett home decorations, oversight of Rental set up

1:30 Rental Shop arrives with bandstand, tables, and chairs

3 pm Setup complete

4pm Band arrives for set up & sound check

4:30 Caterer Arrives

5:45 Photographer arrives Shuttle service begins Tides Folly Beach Hotel to/from Bennett home

6:00 Guests arrive Cocktails begin

6:30 Appetizers light > heavy until

8:00 Band begins

8:12 Sunset champagne toast & Father daughter dance

8 to 11:00 Dance party Open bar.

11:45 Last shuttle to Tides

I just hope that everything goes as planned!!! Does that ever happen? What in the world have I forgotten?

Practiced the research defense in the lab today. It's hard to believe that I found a groundbreaking cure for obesity! My research is going to rock the medical world! Dr. Bath appears to be more interested in smelling my hair and brushing his body across mine than completing work in the lab. Some things haven't changed in two years. Should I file a formal complaint? Maybe after graduation. Guy made the funniest joke about Y2K in class thus far: He asked if our handwritten journals are Y2K compliant or if all of our entries will suddenly disappear at the end of the year? Everyone in the silent research lab broke out into laughter! But that's exactly why I believe that Dr. Bathe insists that we make pen and ink entries in addition to an Excel Spreadsheet. He's paranoid about Y2K and losing all of the data that we have compiled. As Guy left the lab today, he made sounds like the phone line connecting then said "You've Got Mail!" and laughed. Sure enough, I checked my AOL account and he had sent a mysterious email.

Subject: For Your Eyes Only

Body: We need to talk. Meet me tomorrow morning at 8am. Morris Island Lighthouse Trailhead.

Guy

> *What in the world is up with this?*

> *So, she was enamored with Guy Andrews… even had a pet name for him. Ken.* Brooke thought.

> May 14

> *At Washout first! Out-paddled Ryan, King of Folly today! Surely made him angry. Now we are Even Steven for yesterday!!!*

> *But much more important, Met Guy at the park entrance. NEVER seen him so nervous. So mysterious. Saying "Let's just quietly walk for a few minutes." How could I have been so clueless? About a third of the way down the paved path was decorated with beautiful layers of artistic graffiti, which change on a daily basis. Quietly we walked along the blacktop path, until he asked me to close my eyes and guided me several yards farther. When he told me to open my eyes, I saw the heart with Guy Loves Megan written in blue spray paint. Guy Andrews in love with me? No Duh!!! All this time I thought that there was not a chance of a serious relationship. Totally clueless, I just stood dumbfounded, unable to respond. The walk down the paved area to the lighthouse was amazing. Said that the thought of going through life, moving on without me felt empty. That he did love Tori, they had been perfect for each other in high school with Victoria being the beautiful cheerleader and Guy being the quarterback. After his injury late in his senior year, he had begun*

to move on from being the center of attention with Tori. Guy had grown away from her over the last two years. So much to think about! I'm overwhelmed and excited in the same breath. I agreed to think about everything after the graduation party.

May 15, 1999

Can't get Guy out of my mind! Although, I've always loved Guy but was sure to keep my feelings in check. Instead, I convinced myself that he was top-notch best friend material. Considered him to be from too good of a family to consider dating me!

The day before Tori's big graduation! Mine too. But no one has noticed!

Photography hired by Tori. Security from the local police department. Frustrated at the last-minute change. No use arguing with Tori. "Talk to the Hand". She is beyond agitated about everything. She's just being bitchy about every detail. Today she asked Dr. Bennett to transfer the lump sum of cash for the party to her bank account. Told him that she would write out checks to pay each vendor herself. WHATEVER!

The three of us hung out at the beach tonight, listening to the radio and talking. Listened to American Top 40. So glad to have Casey Kasem as host again! I have missed him for the last decade. When he announced Ricky Martin's song Livin' la Vida Loca as the number one, we all jumped around dancing like crazy. Happiest I have ever been! Afraid!

Can't decide between the Bennett Sculpting job offer in Kiawah, which would have a wonderful atmosphere, state of the art everything, catering to wealthy people who want to workout with encouragement; or, the Cardiac Rehab offer in Raleigh, NC. Perform acts of kindness for the medically fragile from all walks of life...

May 16

 I graduated valedictorian! Master's Degree in Exercise Science from The College of Charleston! Tonight was so wonderful!!! Everything went as planned except for that creepy photographer. Looks like crazy Willy Wonka. Every time I turned around, he was there, taking my picture. Later, caught him taking pictures of my surfboard! Was he gonna steal it? I latched it to the top of the Jeep, just in case. Looked a little suspicious to me. After the Father Daughter Dance, I was so happy when Dr. Bennett announced to everyone that he wanted to dance with the class valedictorian and couldn't be prouder if he were my father. We slow-danced to Sweet T and Honey's version of "Sweet Child O' Mine. It was the best dance of my life! Victoria kept brushing me off, so I started tailing Guy. As of right now, I have very contrasting emotions! So incredibly excited about my future with Guy. We just could not stay away from each other at the graduation party. In contrast, Victoria was obviously very upset and kept shooting mean looks my way all night. Says that she's happy for us, but her actions speak otherwise.

24 DRIVE TO SLED

Although Brooke had only seven years of experience as a law enforcement officer, she had an early start to her investigative career. Her high school offered forensic science credits. Not only had Brooke graduated from high school with an eye on law enforcement, she had earned her Bachelors of Science degree from the University of South Carolina, all before she graduated from the SC Criminal Justice Academy. Since her first law enforcement certification, she has continued to earn numerous certifications in multiple branches of forensics. Needless to say, she was no stranger to the processes of gathering and preparing evidence. She reminded herself of the basic rules: Do not contaminate the evidence with my prints or DNA; and do not cross-contaminate the evidence from one item to another.

She studied the spiral notebooks placed on the prepared lab table.

These diaries certainly LOOK circa 1999. Why were these not found earlier? Could Guy Andrews have created these? She was not a forensic handwriting expert, called a graphologist. But she knew just a little about forensic science. With gloves donned, before Brooke sent the notebooks off to the forensic services laboratory in Columbia, SC, she prepared them for transport.

Joleen, who was the eternal optimist, except when she was hangry, nearly skipped into the interview room holding a tripod with gloves on her hands.

"Honey, I'm just gonna bring this in here for you. I know that you are gonna need someone to take the pictures. I like to be prepared." Joleen's sweet voice continued: "I can't believe that he agreed to leave Megan Taylor's diaries here. We didn't even need to get a search warrant..."

"Yet." Brooke interrupted. "We don't need a search warrant, yet. There may be information in these to show "probable cause." Joleen focused and snapped pictures as Brooke turned each page. Later, she would use pictures for comparison. She wanted to be a good evidence custodian by handing the actual paper copies as little as possible. Knowing that she would be waiting for the lab to perform the scientific analysis, she used the opportunity to take a peek. *Just a quick look...* She knew just enough to be dangerous with forensic handwriting analysis. She opened the first of the personal diaries. *Trying to remember... Handwriting analysis... First, determine if it's an original or a copy. Based on the fact that the pages are still attached to the spiral notebook, the ink is blue... appears to be from a ballpoint pen. They look original to me. Second, determine if we are comparing a known sample... Is this a known sample? I would say no... That's what I want to know. Did Megan Taylor write these diaries? Third, determine if the writing is distorted or the same. Doesn't look distorted. It looks the same.*

Brooke, using the gloves, turned several pages. She was looking for any differences in writing style, added paragraphs, or general changes to jump out at her. Now using magnification on her phone camera, she began to look at the details.

These variations in the details are what makes handwriting so unique. It requires not only the knowledge, but the experience of a trained officer to perform document examinations with credible conclusions.

Brooke knew a few terms: letter formations, line quality, alignment and arrangement. She would leave that to the expert. However, she had read the book *Handwriting Analysis: Putting it to Work for You* by Andrea McNichol. This was the first time that she would use the wealth of information for an investigation. She remembered the terms loops, felons, claws, spacing, slant. Indeed, this little peek into the handwritten diaries gave Brooke a smidgen of insight into the author's personality.

Just because I read a book does not make me an expert but, this handwriting angle is slanted to the right. Most likely the author is right-handed. The letter style… the letter "e" is written with even loops; letters are joined grapevines. She would need to wait for the lab results and the associated level of certainty.

She was hopeful for a high level of certainty either way. For instance, the results may read that the author is identified as 100% certain; or the author may be eliminated with 100% certainty. Included would be the level of certainty, it was the nine level scale from *Identification to Elimination.*

With the notebook diaries and the professional journals ready for transport, she placed the documents in the protective container in the trunk of her Sedan along with the wetsuit. She pulled away from headquarters making her way toward Interstate 26 for the hour and a half drive. The six-lane traffic driving west on I-26 required all of Brooke's focus as she merged into 65 mph traffic. Impatient commuters on the roadway frequently changed lanes, making the trip an interactive deadly game for the first twenty miles. She drove in silence with white knuckles before either of them spoke. Finally, Corley broke the silence with obvious sarcasm.

"Why does the Red Mercedes think that it's a smart choice to cross five lanes of traffic to get to the exit for Top Golf?" Corley finally broke the silence. Now the co-workers were both smiling. Brooke joined the sarcasm.

"Exactly... What the heck were they thinking? Oh! Spur of the moment they decided: I need to drop a hundred bucks at Top Golf? Now, that's worth dying for!"

Brooke laughed at Corley and her own quick wit. She needed the laugh, but moreso she needed Corley's company. He always seemed to have a different point of view. Brooke began to relax into the drive a little as they drove past the North Charleston exits. Her thoughts turned back to work.

"Okay, let's talk through Megan Taylor's case. You know it always helps me to talk out loud."

"You go first... Like I have a choice, trapped in the front seat of your car. What do you know?"

"Found strangled and left in the flats. Yeah, so somebody wanted it to look like it was an accidental drowning. But immediately, Palmer and what's-his-face… You know, the one that looks like Gene Wilder's Willy Wonka…"

"What in the world are you talking about?" Corley interrupted. "Willy Wonka?" Brooke glanced at Corley's snickering grin, smiled back and began again.

"Apparently, back in the day…"

"You mean May of 1999?" Corley was clarifying which "day."

"Yes, I've been watching the videos from back in the day… May 16 of 1999, to be specific. Sergeant Palmer had a sidekick that looked like the OG Willy Wonka played by Gene Wilder… What's his name…? Wainwright. That's it! Wainwright was the videographer."

Brooke was excited to have remembered his name. She momentarily thought about the now plump parasitic brain sucker that has been residing in her low bun when her thoughts were interrupted by Corely again.

"I know that the timing is poor, but I have to ask… When you watched the videos, could you see through the clothing?"

"Really, Corley?" They both laughed until Brooke realized that she was having too much fun. Somehow, she felt obligated to be alert, serious, and somber while "on a case".

"The answer is no. I could not see through Sergeant Palmer's or Detective Wainwright's clothing. Oh, or the 911 caller, he had on a wetsuit but I couldn't see through his clothes either."

"Really? Then why the recall?" Corley sounded

disappointed.

"Do you suppose that it could have been a huge marketing ploy to announce a recall of home video cameras that had x-ray night vision. Recall a product because it was too good?"

"Really? You think that it was a big marketing idea?" Corley's voice sounded disappointed with the thought of deception by Sony.

"I don't think so... Not back then." Corley finally disagreed.

"Back to the case. Megan Taylor was found in the flats. Her autopsy revealed that she was strangled by asphyxiation with ligature marks and defensive injuries. Did I tell you that she had broken fingers that happened pre-mortem?"

"Ah, yes. As I remember, you also mentioned the nail clippings as we waited for our dinner. How appetizing. You are all work. Does that brain ever stop thinking about this case?"

"That's another no." Without taking a moment to transition, Brooke continued to talk to her vehicle-captive audience. "I brought the wetsuit that Megan was wearing when she died. I mean when she was murdered. I expect to find some DNA from Megan and Ryan Willis on her wetsuit. But I'm hoping to find someone else's DNA on there. Someone who already has a DNA profile in CODIS."

The acronym was for the Combined DNA Index System. It's the FBI software that matches DNA profiles to known and unknown samples. Over the last several decades, the software has helped local, state, and national officers apply scientific technology to solve active and cold cases. If someone had previously been convicted of a felony or was involved in an unsolved case; their DNA could generate a match.

"We could have an answer soon." Corley sounded reassuring.

So glad that he's with me.

They drove in silence past the never-ending Loblolly pine trees and the occasional billboard. After passing a large billboard that read "Jesus, Save My Soul." Corley broke the silence "Wonder who pays for those billboards…"

"I have no clue but I've pondered that too!"

"Speaking of pondering, how are things with you and Jake?" It was unusual for Corley to ask about her relationships. He usually just endured the subject when Brooke brought it up.

"Well, I don't know. He's so nice. He is so easy to get along with… And you know how I feel about his dog, Diesel. It's all good. Why do you ask? Did you hear something? Know something that I don't?"

"Oh no, nothing like that. Just asking. You know. Passing time." Corely was quiet for the remainder of the ride, and Brooke remained in deep thought as she exited the interstate and then continued to drive the prints to the SLED Lab in Columbia, South Carolina.

Once inside the lab, donned with safety glasses and gloves, Brooke observed as the professional attempted to lift prints from the notebooks. She used the technique often helpful with older prints on porous surfaces like paper, called ninhydrin treatment. Shaking the spray bottle, the technician mixed ninhydrin with acetone, then sprayed the pages that looked most covered in doodles around the diary entries.

Oh, makes sense that the pages with the most doodles may have the most fingerprints. If Guy's story is legit, I'd expect to see a combination of Megan's and Guy's fingerprints. If there are only Guy's prints, it may indicate that he falsified the entries and these are not Megan's words. The downside to the technique is that it usually takes several days for the mixture to dry on the paper to reveal the Rheumanns purple fingerprints.

No need to wait here. Brooke drove the hour and a half back to headquarters. She reluctantly returned to her makeshift office. Now she took the time to read the entries in the professional journals obtained from Dr Bob Bathe's home office. She began with the week before Megan's murder. Nothing interesting except a few entries written on the signature pages.

25 DR BOB BATHE HQ

Dr Bob Bathe had been invited to headquarters to provide information on the professional journals obtained during the search of his home office. Law enforcement had obtained the professional journals from May of 1999. The handwritten notes by Megan Taylor were relevant because they provide a known handwriting sample.

Brooke began the Interview at Headquarters.

"Did you have anything to do with the murder of Megan Taylor?" Brooke was straight to the point. This time she wanted Dr. Bath to feel uncomfortable.

The more uncomfortable, the better. That was why she had asked him to come to headquarters for the interview.

Last time, we were on his turf. This time mine.

With his back to the corner, Dr. Bathe reacted as if he had been slapped in the face with a fish. Surprise filled his face and his hands flew up into the air in a defensive posture.

"Of course not! Why would you say such a thing?"

"Why else would you put yourself at risk for being arrested for obstruction of justice? Why else would you keep the professional journals from law enforcement... That is, unless you have a bigger secret to hide."

"What do you mean? Am I under arrest?" The

previously nefarious man now looked as if he would burst into tears. Detective Mason began to explain in detail:

"There is probable cause that you are obstructing justice by interfering with the investigation of the homicide of Megan Taylor. You are not under arrest at this time. Instead, we are hoping for your cooperation."

The change in location from your comfy home to my bleak interview room must have helped you to better understand the gravity of the situation.

"What is it that you want to know?" Brooke was silent as she flipped through documents on her laptop. Next, she took a sip of her coffee before beginning to share the information on the screen.

"While executing the search warrant at 1544 E Ashley Avenue of your entire premises to include but not limited to vehicles, residences, sheds and out structures associated with the address, we obtained professional journals dated May 1999. Most of those entries were handwritten by Megan Taylor. Does that sound familiar?"

"You don't understand. It's not what you think!

"This is a direct quote from Megan Taylor: Bathe comes in and acts as if HE has completed the research, analyzed the data, and discovered the microbe! Can't believe that he is trying to convince the entire team that HE is responsible for the new discovery!'"

Brooke was holding the professional Journal that she had been denied while visiting his home. She placed it on the table for Dr. Bath to read and then waited for an answer…

"Okay, it is true that *we* discovered a previously unidentified microbe whose primary source of energy is obtained by consuming lipid stores in its host. However, we had very different views on how to proceed. She instantly wanted to attempt to create an injectable version of the microbe for consumer weight loss." Dr. Bath cleared his throat, removed his glasses, and began to clean them as he continued.

"I was much more cautious, as we needed more research on the long-term effects of the microbes on the various systems of the human body."

"Certainly, sounds like a motive to me!" Corley obviously chose to be the adversary in the interview today. "Can you imagine how many people would pay to get a shot of Megan's fat remover? I'm thinking there were millions of dollars to be made." He crossed his arms over his chest as if to add emphasis to his statement.

"What about this entry by another student that says, and I quote: 'Stop your hair sniffing or else! I told you before to leave Megan alone!'"
Again, Dr Bob Bath had a strong reaction. This time it was as if he had been struck by lightning. His entire body shook in a high frequency vibration for a brief moment before he regained his composure.

"That never happened! It's a common practice in research to look over someone's shoulder to look in a microscope." He weakly held his matter-of-fact poise.

"How about this entry from Megan's personal diary, 'getting concerned about being alone in the lab with the creep! Keeps sneaking up behind me. Freaking me out!!'"

26 MORRIS LIGHTHOUSE

"I was totally in love with Megan Taylor!!! Just four days before her death, I told her!" Joleen gasped out loud in disbelief as Guy Andrews defended his innocence.

"Really?! Now, don't you understand my point of view? It does look suspicious." Joleen's twangy drawl sounded as sweet as muscadine wine. However, the words spoken were at tart as an unripe persimmon.

He leaned forward, throwing his hands into the air. "It's true! She met me at the Morris Lighthouse. As we walked along the paved path near the trailhead, I started to point out some of the graffiti art. Just laughing and kidding around. She didn't know that the prior night I took some blue paint… painted a heart and painted, "Megan will you marry me?"

"She was silent. She didn't answer… I confessed to Megan for the first time that I was totally in love with her… Found her to be the most amazing person I have ever met. I longed to be with her and couldn't stand the thought of being away from her…"

Guy explained how they finished the paved path and walked through the heavy dunes side by side. He talked seriously about the future they had together. Holding hands, they watched as the tide lowered around the lighthouse revealing today's ocean treasures. Looking for shells side by side at the back of Rat Island, they had their very first kiss, under the artwork "eyes."

The eyes were painted on the concrete bridge pier and overlook the inlet.

"We held hands as we walked back to the Jeep, then we made love for the first time. We agreed to keep it a secret until after graduation."

Brooke pushed the issue, "Well, why did you keep it a secret?"

"We didn't want any drama to interfere with our celebration. Megan wanted the three of us to graduate that afternoon, then for Victoria to be the center of celebration for her graduation party later that evening. She didn't want the guests to be talking about the two of us. That's what Megan told me moments before making love. That we keep it on the down low until after Victoria has her night."

"Did you tell anyone?"

Still unable to stop the cracking of his voice, Guy Andrews nodded his head "yes" and began again "It was after the party that Meg and I told Victoria."

"How did she take the news?"

"Not so good. First it was disbelief, then it was anger. She told us all the reasons that things wouldn't work out yet she acted as if she was happy for us, but I could see her body language. Definitely angry."

Palmer appeared at the door of Brooke's makeshift office. He handed her a paper and left the room. Brooke excused herself allowing Joleen to finish the interview.

The results from Megan Taylor's diary ninhydrin analysis revealed multiple right thumb, index and middle finger prints. Most of the prints were a match for

Megan Taylor. Her prints were obtained at the time of her autopsy. Other index and thumb prints were found to be a match for Guy Andrews. He voluntarily submitted fingerprints and provided a DNA swab after his interview.

As for the handwriting analysis, the results indicated with 98 percent certainty that the handwriting from Dr. Bathe's research journals and the handwriting in personal diaries Guy brought to headquarters were written by the same author, Megan Taylor.

So, it appears that Megan did write the diary entries… And that Guy Andrews' story is holding up as true… So far. It also means that Dr. Bathe was a hair sniffer after all.

27 DIESEL ON CENTER STREET

Brooke, Jacob and Diesel walked down Palmetto Blvd towards Center Street. Wearing his silver studded collar, Diesel, the 105-pound Rottweiler was looking especially handsome. Strutting on the leash, his shiny coat and big smile attracted dog lovers. Others, alarmed by his size, crossed the street. The perfect specimen for his breed, it was his wide chest and defined muscles that made him the great protector. Although some may find him intimidating, for Brooke it was love at first sight. He was a gentle giant whose eyes were full of loyalty. Now standing under the outdoor tiki bar, Diesel loudly lapped up the fresh water from the always present doggie bowl. After his fill of fresh water, Diesel sprawled himself on the floor. Jacob tightly secured the leash around the concrete pylon. "Perfect! See, we still made it in time to get seats in the shade."

Brooke joined in on the mood, while smiling she agreed, "Perfect day for a beer at the Folly Beach Crab Shack!" Brooke was elated to be able to face the sidewalk during the "crabby hour drink specials." The coastal SC afternoon sun can be brutal on our eyes and skin. However, the sun's heat on Big D's black fur or forcing his paws on hot pavement were simply abuse. Relieved that Big D was shaded, she ordered a Blue Moon beer and tried to turn off her brain. "Running to the ladies' room."

"Don't run. It's Folly happy hour."

She smiled and kissed Jacob's cheek. "Yes, it is." Brooke knew that she needed to transition from work mode.

Once inside the restaurant, she was reminded that the place had not changed or been updated in the last 20 years. *Love it!* She agreed with the premise that Folly required commitment from its residents to remain the same Folly.

Seeing herself in the mirror… *No need to feed that imaginary starving brain sucker.* Brooke freed her blonde hair from the low bun, her "go to" professional look. Instantly feeling liberated, she looked into the mirror while she braided her wavy hair and secured it on the left with an elastic band. Perfect finishing touch to her purple gauze mini dress, flip flops and juicy couture backpack. *Now I'm ready for Folly time!*

She stepped back outside and gave Diesel a reassuring whisper…" Good boy, Big Diesel. " before taking a sip of her beer.

Each day during happy (or crabby) hour 4-7 pm, the sidewalks are filled with smiling people who stroll in and out of shops like Folly Sol carrying unique treasures from local artisans. Others laugh with families over ice cream. Locals and visitors alike enjoy the wonderful restaurants along Center Street. It was early evening, yet one would never know by the number of people dressed in swimsuits, cover ups, T-shirts and flip-flops. Definitely appropriate dress code for the outdoor seating establishments on Folly. Most local drivers avoid

Center Street which is filled with distracted pedestrians jaywalking into traffic. The oblivious vacationers dart into traffic like the Frogger game, risking their lives to get a better look at a surfboard or to eat a pineapple smoothie.

Brooke loved to bar-hop the live music scene at the various hangouts. All within walking distance of Tides Hotel and most of the rental homes, Folly definitely has a beach town atmosphere. Surrounded by the culture, Brooke was able to slip into the vibe after her first beer.

Before she ordered her second, she suddenly realized that she had forgotten to eat. She made her way to the oyster bar when she noticed a lone guy sitting on the barstool, playing the guitar and singing. *He looks familiar.* She remembered these mid-fifties fella from the other morning on the beach. He had given her a head nod from a distance, just before her jog. However, this time he was more familiar. Something about his bright blue eyes, Brooke was drawn to them several times as he sang "Cheeseburger in Paradise". The sun-drenched singer finished the song and began to speak. "Thank y'all for comin' out tonight. I'm dedicating this next one to someone that I lost a long time ago... This one's for you, Meg!" He began to strum the guitar as he sang to the tune of the famous song: "Yesterday, all your troubles seemed so far away; Now it looks as if you washed away. Oh, I believe you were washed away…" She waited for her Chilled Blue Crab Dip and Hushpuppy basket. Hearing the altered lyrics of the familiar song, she recognized the 911 caller from decades earlier, Ryan Willis.

Immediately, upon recognizing Ryan, Brooke's brain returned to work mode. *Can't believe he's been here on Folly this entire time.* She retrieved a card from her backpack and wrote on the back, "Remember Megan Taylor? Visit my table." Brooke wrapped the note in a $20 bill and waited for an opportunity to pass the message. Hardly able to contain herself, she thrust the bill into the hands of the singer while the patrons clapped. Song over and message delivered, Brooke flip-flopped away as if she had just provided a tip for a requested song. Taking her seat at the table next to Ryan, Brooke placed the blue crab dip in the center of the wooden table. "Hope that you're hungry! 'Cause I need help with this delicious crab dip."

"Darn right! Let me see for myself" He took a bite of crab dip, "Yep, you are right! Delicious!" Jacob nodded towards Ryan, "What song did you request?"

Brooke wanted it to look like she was requesting a song. She hadn't actually thought of a song to request as her cover. Quickly thinking, "Surprise! I asked him to come to our table. I figured you'd have a song picked out before he gets here. You better come up with a good one, I tipped him really well!"

"Brooke, thanks! That's really nice. Let me think of something." Jacob was smiling as if he had been awarded a grand prize at a surfing competition. "I love that about you!

As soon as Ryan Willis approached the table, Jacob began first, "Do you know, Buffett, A Pirate Looks At Forty?"

Ryan didn't question a thing, he just played along with Brook. "Yeah, One of my favorites. You got it." Ryan looked down at the rottweiler, "Mind if I pet your dog?"

Jacob looked like a proud parent, "Sure he's friendly."

Ryan leaned to Megan and whispered, "Meet me at the County Park at sunrise if you want to blow Megan Taylor's case wide open."

28 BREAK

Folly Beach County Park
1100 W Ashley Ave, Folly Beach, SC 29439
"You show up in uniform? Really?"

Ryan Willis' face was filled with anxiety as he whispered through his clenched teeth into Brooke's window.

"Do you have a problem with me being in uniform?"

Brooke was taken back by his criticism. He had seemed so laid-back last night at The Shack. He continued to speak in a whisper through clenched teeth. He looked so upset that Brooke thought that he may walk away.

"I thought that when I asked to meet here at the park, that you'd get the hint. I was thinkin' you'd be here in shorts and a t-shirt sitting over there at the snack bar... or over there on the beach with two chairs. Instead, you show up in a gun-totin' uniform with a marked car parked beside the guard gate. This is exactly why I didn't want to meet you anywhere else on the island. You are just not very discrete."
Brooke ignored his tongue lashing about the uniform and listened as he continued,

"What kind of detective are you, anyhow? And I have a reputation to uphold, ya know. Don't want to ruin my music career. Locals see me talkin' to you, they're gonna be wondering what's up."

Brooke wanted to appease Ryan. She needed the information that Ryan had said last night: Meet me at the Folly County Park when it opens, if you want to "crack the case wide open." He had been on the island for all of these years. Hanging out at the bars with the locals... *Ryan would be the perfect informant, if I can gain his trust.*

"I'll change into my workout clothes and meet you on the beach near the rock jetty." Immediately relief filled his face before Ryan Willis flip flopped away from the car. Now Brooke began to survey the area before gathering her backpack and using the private changing area. Relieved to have a place to transform from Superman into Clark Kent, she used the private changing room to turn from law enforcement officer into a nosey vacationer. Now wearing athletic shorts and a Lost Dog Café T-Shirt, Brooke exited the changing room after concealing her secret can of whoop-ass: pepper spray!

Not expecting to use my can of whoop-ass today. Nevertheless, readily accessible if I need it.

Now walking barefoot through the sandy path, she topped the crest of the dune and completed her ritual. Facing the sun, she paused for a quick second to capture the warmth on her face. She exhaled all of her anxiety slowly and completely until she felt that her lungs were on the verge of collapse. Abruptly she inhaled as much of the salty breeze into her lungs as possible. At one with the beach, she began to quickly stroll past the seagrasses intertwined with bright yellow and orange flowers. Now on the firm sand of the beach, she began to jog. She passed the beachgoers basking in the sun and the beachcombers with eyes turned downwards for shells, she broke into a jog. Making her way towards the jetty, her thoughts returned to Ryan Willis.

What kinda information does he know? Is it gossip? Something he saw first-hand? Maybe he was involved? I'm about to find out. Gotta play it safe.

She continued to jog on the firm sand towards the jetty. She could see Ryan ahead reaching down into the tidepools between the rocks. As Brooke neared the jetty, Ryan sat up, having retrieved a starfish from between the rocks. Still holding the sea creature in his hands, he presented it for Brooke to inspect as if he was wanting to share the extremely unusual experience with her. Gently, he placed the five fingered star into the ocean and quietly watched its retreat into deeper waters.

Brooke interrupted the silence. "What do you know about Megan Taylor?"

Immediately Ryan looked up from the water to see Brooke. "I still pay my respects each week when I sing 'Yesterday… Meg was just washed away'. How long ago now?"

"It's been 23 years."

"That's why I changed the lyrics of the song… Everyone else moved on with their lives. Not me. Spending every day on my surfboard in the place where it happened… with lots of time to think. Dude, she was here every day! Thought that I met my surfin' soul-mate... Then they murdered her. Left her on the beach… let her memory be washed away. Not me, I'll never forget her."

"Ryan, who would want to forget her?" Brooke, still acting her part and trying to sound more like the friendly vacationer than the lead investigator of a homicide."

"People around Folly. Suspicious ya know, like not wanting any law enforcement sniffin' around the locals. We keep to ourselves and mind our own business here." Quiet again, Ryan walked away from the jetty towards the far end of the beach. Brooke broke into a jog to catch up with him.

"I'm not a snitch." Ryan whispered as she began to walk beside him.

"Not asking you to be a snitch here, just asking you to be honest about what you know."

"Yeah, well there's a pact amongst us locals. We don't rat each other out. Especially to outsiders." At the word 'outsider', Brooke reacted as if she had been gut punched. She had lived on Folly Island for the last seven years!

Really, I'm still an outsider? Glancing to Ryan, she looked to the source of her hurt. He must have read her mind.

"No! Not you. You ARE a local. Seen you around here over the years." He cleared his throat and spoke just loud enough for Brooke to clearly hear him. "Quiet observation is my thing. I just blend into the background. People drink. People talk. People POP. You've seen the endless hype about Live, Laugh, Love. I see it firsthand every day."

Glad for Ryan to become loose-lipped, she

encouraged him to continue his story. "Say that again... Drink, talk, and what?"

She stopped walking and directly faced him. He was facing her, looking into the sun. Brooke disguised as the jogger could see the sun shining directly onto the smooth tan skin of his face and reflecting off of his sandy silver hair.

With a serious tone and loud enough to escape the sound of the crashing waves, Ryan repeated himself, "People drink, People talk, People POP. Meaning: Piss on Other People."

Not what she had expected Ryan to say. "What? I don't understand... Literally or figuratively?"

"No! Not like a dog. But, more like, talking trash about other people." Ryan looked at her, as if waiting for Brooke's lightbulb to shine above her head.

"Oh! I get it. Drink, talk, POP!" Brooke was louder than she had expected to overcome the sounds of the inlet waves crashing against the shore.

"Fer sure. Only, my motto is drink, talk, and stop before you POP!"

They both smiled. Brooke felt her gut relax for the first time since the conversation started. "Come on Ryan, I'm not asking you to share gossip or to rat out anyone. Just tell me the facts. Only things that you know firsthand."

"Firsthand?"

"Only tell me the things that you have seen with your eyes... Just the facts. Not gossip."

Ryan took a deep breath, looked down at his feet, and began to speak quickly as he expelled the secret that had burned his soul for so many years.

"It was the next day that Murphy Wainwright came up to me outta nowhere at the Lost Dog and sat at my table. Told me to meet him outside. Sure 'nuff, when I came outside, he was sitting at the bench in the memorial garden. You know, the one between the library and the Lost Dog. Never forget his first words... 'If you know what's good for ya, you'll let this all wash away... like the tide. You get my drift?' I told him "No", I don't understand. He said "Exactly! You don't understand. It's much more complex than you could possibly understand. But you gotta trust me that It's best for Folly. I remember him tellin' me not to talk to the cops. Saying that we keep our secrets on the island. I really didn't know what to think. But I wondered what in the world Megan's murder had to do with him! I was so curious that I kept my eyes and ears open. Saw that woman. You know, the one that looks like she dutton belong here on Folly... I saw 'em together at the park. Not this one, the other park, the one on the river, near the bridge. Watched him hand her pictures. Ya know. back then we all took real pictures."

"What happened?"

"Well, she was crying as she looked at 'em. Murphy had to be very patient before she calmed down enough to write a check. Saw her with my own eyes, take out her checkbook. We used checks back then too."

"Well, what was the check payment for?"

"I don't know. I'm guessing the pictures and whatever he did to get them. But it was the next morning that I found Megan floating in the flats. Didn't make the connection until later that morning when Murphy shoved an evidence bag into my hand and said, 'Destroy this!'". That's when I knew that he was somehow involved."

"Wait. Really! You think that Murphy, the Save the Turtles Foundation leader is involved in Megan Taylor's murder? Did you destroy the evidence bag?"

Ryan staring down at his flip flops, "Folly is a small place. Word got around real fast that I found the body. After I told the story a few times, he told me that Detective Palmer was an outsider. And that if I need to talk about Megan Taylor, I should talk to him instead of Palmer."

Brooke couldn't wait any longer, "What about the evidence? Did you destroy it?"

Completely ignoring her questions, Ryan, still staring at his flip flops continued, "The foundation was started shortly afterwards…Over the years, I saw him around. It was like he kept being drawn to me. Always wanted to know if Palmer had been asking around about Megan's murder. All I know is that I've never wanted to forget about Megan and I never wanted to POP."

It was all that Brooke could do to contain herself, "Ryan, what the hell happened to the evidence bag?"

Hearing his name, Ryan reluctantly looked up at Brooke, "If you want to know what happened to Megan Taylor, you'll have to ask Murphy. I didn't see anything. But if you want the evidence bag to make him talk, meet me at 1520 East Ashley at daybreak. Murphy will be patrolling the beach there, looking for the baby turtles. Yeah, with the renourishment project this year, he's out there every morning. See you in the morning." Ryan turned and flip-flopped away faster than anyone she had ever seen. *Definitely a professional flip-flopper.*

Brooke protested, "What the hell? Don't flip-flop away from me!"

Ryan turned and shouted. "Can't wait to see you in the morning for the surfing lesson." Quickly, he turned back around, and flip-flopped away faster. Disguised as a jogger, she began to run and easily caught up to Ryan.

"Just meet me beside the pavilion steps. You know, where they hold the Wahine Classic. Stand beside the community bulletin board."

"What the hell?"

"Gotta trust me on this one. If we are going to be working and spending time together. The locals gotta see a reason. Surf lessons. Get it."

Brooke couldn't believe the words coming out of Ryan's mouth. *Working and spending time together.* "Oh, Surf lessons, I get it."

"Your first lesson is in the morning at daybreak. Be dressed for your lesson… Mason… Can I call you Mason?"

"Well, if I'm taking surf lessons, call me Brooke. I'll see you in the morning." Wanting to have the last word, Brooke began to jog away.

29 COMMUNITY BOARD

Dressed in a navy and floral RipCurl spring suit, Brooke waited under the street light at 1520 East Ashley as instructed by Ryan. Last night, she remembered his words, *working and spending time together.* She really wanted to believe Ryan's story about the involvement of the community leader, Murphy Wainwright. *It just doesn't make sense.* Not trusting anyone, Brooke was prepared. Just in case she needed protection this morning, she held her purple Juicy Couture backpack with her hand on her revolver and Corley was parked in his sedan less than 30 feet away. Brooke was beginning to wonder if Ryan would show up or if he had set her up to disappear. When he flip-flopped his way from the darkness and into the misty morning light.

Ryan didn't greet Brooke but continued to pass her as he began to speak. "Before I tell you everything, I have something to show you." Ryan reached into his pocket to withdraw a keyring. Using the small, oddly-shaped key, he unlocked the community communication board. Brooke was expecting him to produce a trifold map, followed by a cautionary spill about the dangers of surfing, followed by surfing etiquette. Information, all of which Brooke had "surfed the internet" last night, consuming everything she could to prepare for her "surf lesson." Instead, he pulled the corner of the cork, behind it was a hinge. Ryan quickly pulled on a small handle made of driftwood. The door, behind the now removed cork board, opened. The empty space inside was not empty. It contained a sealed

evidence bag
which contained a green Mountain Dew bottle.

30 MURPHY'S RECALL

As predicted by Ryan Willis, Brooke could recognize the shadow of Murphy Wainwright on the beach just before daylight. She jogged over to him and asked that he meet her in front of the Tides Hotel. Now sitting on the beach, Brooke asked details about the days leading up to Megan Taylor's murder. Murphy recalled how he had tailed Guy Andrews. He had been hired to do so by Victoria Bennett and had been paid well to "provide surveillance with photographs of Guy Andrews until further notice." He remembered the first meeting very well. It had been his demise. He remembered how it had all started…

"You see, back then…"

"When do you mean? 1999?" Brooke clarified.

"Yes, it was May of 1999. I was working as an investigative photographer for law enforcement and doing wedding photography as a side hustle. But my passion was and still is saving our sea creatures. Specifically, our loggerhead turtles. Having grown up on Folly, I totally could see the changes happening. I could see that our beach was changing. With more and more surfers coming to the area, they were attracting people to our beach. These observers of the surfing community were bringing problems for the turtles. Not the surfers themselves. They seem to be at one with nature… very aware of the importance of leaving the island as they found it. However, as I said, it was all of the observers, the beachgoers, the partyers that would leave the beach cluttered with bottles, beach blankets, beer cans, beach chairs. It became my mission to start a sea turtle awareness program. Remember, it was 1999. No one knew the negative impact that beach goers were having on the sea turtle population. At the time, I had been trying to tell the locals by word of mouth. They listened, but with so many guests to the island each week, we needed something formal to educate more people. I knew that we needed money to fund a Save the Sea Turtles non-profit. We needed a concerted effort to educate the public, sweep the beaches, and protect the sea turtles. My focus was to earn money as quickly as possible to increase awareness of the dwindling sea turtle populations. So, I started doing photography on the side to raise money. Everything I earned on the side was donated to start the Save the Sea Turtles Foundation.

"What does this have to do with your involvement with Megan Taylor's murder? Get to the point." Brooke was becoming very impatient and it showed in her tone.

"It's very relevant, as you will see. Now, where was I? Oh yeah, I was down at the chapel on West Indian… You know the one… I had run a $75 special for May weddings and was booked every weekend that month. I remember that I had just finished a four-hour ordeal for $75. That was my all-inclusive wedding photo package at the Folly Beach Church Chapel back then. I charged $100 for the beach package because there are no golf carts allowed on the beach. Had to carry all of my photography equipment through the sand and use a tripod on the beach."

"Okay, so you were telling us how you met Victoria Bennett?"

"Yeah. After the wedding, like a spirit, she appeared behind me. Like creepy, outta nowhere and casually asked: "Are you the wedding photographer who also does security?". Not saying anything, I spun around to see the source of the voice. The beautiful woman in stiletto heels handed me a check for $5000. That was ten times the monthly rent of my island efficiency. Victoria, much like today, looked very out of place. I was struck by how she looked like Hollywood had come to Folly. Before I could say anything else, she made an offer that I had to consider. You see, this was enough money to make my sea turtle non-profit dream come true. Victoria told me to see the note on the check, "Officially, I'm hiring you to provide the photography for the graduation party. This is your deposit or retainer fee, if you prefer." My eyes were as large as saucers when I looked at the check and back at the woman standing behind me, 'You will receive additional money after the event.'" That's what Victoria Bennett had said when she approached me about the photography gig at the graduation party on May 16. 'Until then, you are unofficially hired to provide surveillance with photographs of Guy Andrews until further notice.'"

After taking a sip from his Stanley cup he continued. "So, Yes! I cashed the check. I considered it a blessing at the time. A good start for the Sea Turtle

Foundation. Happy for the "windfall", I began to tail Guy. It's pretty easy on the island. I just drove parallel but one block away as he made his way down W Ashley Avenue. Guy was driving his sedan and I was in the golf cart. When he parked at the trailhead to the Morris Lighthouse, a girl came up to him. They started to talk then walked down towards the light house. I spent hours hiding in the sweet grass and behind the scrub oaks. I waited and waited for them to return from Morris Lighthouse." He took another sip from his cup, "I was able to snap a few pictures while sitting on my electric golf cart as they entered the trail. My electric golf cart was quiet. It allowed me to effectively trail Guy Andrews. As they started toward Morris Lighthouse, I saw nothing suspicious, two college friends taking a walk. After waiting for over an hour in my golf cart, I was bored. So, I walked over and began to take pictures of the art on the paved areas of the trail. Sure nuff, they came walking back and caught me off guard. I just continued to take pictures. As they approached me, they greeted me and walked by holding hands. Of course I began to secretly take pictures. When they stopped, Guy got on one knee and pointed to the spray-painted words "Megan, will you marry me?" Later I got a shot of that too. Discreetly, I followed them to Guy's sedan and caught pictures of them kissing and hugging goodbye. Definitely a lingering, loving embrace. Not a friendship kiss, ya know?"

"Okay, so you caught Guy Andrews proposing and kissing someone..." Brooke was trying to move the relevance of the story along.

"Later that night, I met Victoria at the park. I showed her the pictures of Guy Andrews kissing the girl, the painted words on the Morris Lighthouse trail, and the pictures of them going into a small efficiency apartment. At first, she cried, then she became angry. She wrote me a check for another $5,000 and told me that the gig for the graduation party and morning after would bring another $20,000. She added that to keep it legit, the check would be written to the foundation. I was beyond ecstatic. Finally, I would have the money needed to create the Sea Turtle Conservation Foundation for Folly. I didn't know what she expected in return. Really, I didn't care. I believed that she wanted my discreet surveillance services and was dedicated to my foundation."

"Well, I'm assuming that was not the case?"

"No! She is definitely not a special friend to the sea turtles. I would describe her more as an osprey, you know the large bird of prey. And like a fish in the ocean, I was totally unaware of the dangers of Victoria. She was like an osprey swooping down to catch an off-guard barracuda, me, in her clutches. She began to devour me before I even realized that she was a predator.

"Oh, so you are claiming to be the victim here?"

"For sure! I AM the victim."

"Not sure that you can claim to be the victim when Megan Taylor was murdered?"

"We were both victims of Victoria."

"Yet somehow you are alive and she is not!"

"Yes, true. But listen to me first, then make your

judgments."

"Go on. Continue with your side of the story."

"Where was I? Oh yeah. So, I was hired by Victoria to photograph her College of Charleston graduation party. It was nothing unusual, I took lots of pictures of classmates hugging, drinking, dancing… you know, celebrating. I remember Victoria offering me a drink at the end of the night. I woke up with her standing over me several hours later, she was standing over me holding my video camera. That's when I realized that I had been drugged. While under the influence of something in that drink, Victoria began to convince me that Megan Taylor was the only thing standing between me and my foundation. That Megan Taylor was a terrible person, that she needed to disappear. And that she agreed with me. The sea turtles needed my help. While under the influence of something in the Mountain Dew bottle, I followed her sick plan. We went to the beach and waited for Megan. I watched her untangle a turtle trapped in a beach chair. Then I attacked Megan. I strangled her with her surfboard leash. What I didn't realize at the time, was that Victoria used the tripod to video the entire murder. She's used it to keep me quiet all these years. Threatening to share the video publicly. Given the choice at hand, I chose silence and sea turtles." Murphy Wainwright acted as if he would make the same choice again. As if he had absolved himself because he had saved so many sea creatures over the last twenty-three years. Holding his shoulders back and his head high, he took a sip of water from his Stanley cup and continued,

"It was the very next day; the foundation received the money and I received an offer to be the founding member of the "Save the Turtle Foundation." You know, over time, I just couldn't imagine the embarrassment of the video leak. Call me shallow, but I agreed to the offer. Victoria has had her talons in me ever since. You see, it's not as it appeared. Megan and I were BOTH victims that morning. It's just that I survived to fulfill my dream. I've dedicated my life to trying to justify in my mind that Megan would have sacrificed her life if she had known all of the sea turtles that she would ultimately save. Sad, I don't even believe it myself." His voice cracked and he finally broke down and began to sob into his hands. He sat and sobbed, body bouncing between breaths, he didn't speak for several minutes.

Suddenly worried that Murphy Wainwright may have a weapon, Brooke assumed a defensive posture. With her right hand on her weapon inside her backpack, she spoke with authority, "Put your hands on the back of your head and step backwards slowly."

Immediately, Wainwright followed her instructions. With his hands behind his head, Brooke placed her handcuffs around his wrists. He protested, "No, you don't understand!"

"For both of our safety, you are being handcuffed and placed in the back of Officer Corley's car. He will take you to HQ for questioning."

Officer Corley instantly joined the apprehension of Murphy Wainwright. "Nice and slow. No fast movements." Corley patted him down, finding no weapons, he motioned for Wainwright to walk towards the car.

"Wait! Don't take him away just yet." Brooke was still curious, "Why are you smiling about the Mountain Dew bottle?"

"Ryan kept that Mountain Dew bottle. Been in that evidence bag since May 16, 1999. Kept it hidden all of these years." Wainwright was grinning as if he had just won the grand prize.

"Why? Why would you be happy about the Mountain Dew bottle with your prints on it?" Brooke donned gloves from her backpack as she spoke to Wainwright.

Slowly and confidently, Murphy Wainwright snickered out loud, "You see, Detective Mason, the bottle not only has my fingerprints. It also has Victoria Bennett's fingerprints because she handed me the bottle to drink." Still smiling at Brooke while Corley held his handcuffs. "You don't get it yet, do you?"

Brooke with gloves on both hands reached into the compartment behind the corkboard and pulled the corner of the 23-year-old evidence bag. It appeared to be sealed. As a precaution, she placed it into a new evidence bag. She felt the weight of the green bottle. There was liquid in the bottle. The shock on her face must have been evident to Wainwright.

Now sitting on the sidewalk, still in cuffs with Corley standing over him, Murphy began, "Is that a glimmer of an idea? Do you know why I'm happy that Ryan kept the bottle with both our prints? Because she poisoned that, Mountain Dew?" He looked very proud of himself.

"You believe that the Mountain Dew in this bottle from 23 years ago contains a drug that gave you a momentary lapse in judgment to murder Megan Taylor by strangulation in cold blood, just as she was about to begin her life! Do you really believe it?"

"Am I under arrest? Because I think I need an attorney."

31 MARSHA, MARSHA, MARSHA

Victoria drove from downtown Charleston out to Folly to meet her father for breakfast. Over the last 20 years, since moving away from her father's home, she had driven the route many times. As she turned from Calhoun Street onto Highway 30, she began to look across the Ashley River. The marinas along the shores were filled with boats of all shapes and sizes. She remembered her father telling her *"The guy in the 15-foot John boat is having just as much fun as the guy on the 50-foot yacht. No matter the size of the boat, everyone has fun on the water."*

She began to think about her childhood. She and her father had traveled from downtown Charleston to Folly each afternoon while he imparted his wisdom all those years ago. How she had taken her father's advice to act like a lady but think like a man. She had thought like a man when she hired someone to take care of her problem. And had acted like a lady by being discreet with the entire agreement. Glad that she and her accomplice were able to keep the secret for all of these years. At the end of Highway 30, Victoria turned left onto Folly Road. *Don't know why Daddy wants to stay out here on Folly. Look at these people. Everybody West Ashley moves too slowly.*

Now, as she approached the causeway, she looked to the right to see the Folly Beach Boat. The boat had become a tourist attraction after it washed ashore during hurricane Hugo back in 1989. After the devastation to the island, the boat was used as a means of communication to find loved ones. Today it displays "professional graffiti" to wish locals happy birthday or, like today, propose marriage. "Becky, Will you marry me?" was painted in bright blue bubble letters outlined in black. The contrast of the white vessel made the message easy to read against the white background of the vessel.

Feeling sorry for all the guys who are dating gals named Becky. You never know what you will see on Folly.

Next, she passed Crosby's Fish & Shrimp and was to see a glimpse of the boats unloading today's catch. Now crossing the causeway, she saw the many tourists walking along the park to her left and the sidewalk to her right. Families dressed in brightly colored t-shirts holding hands and pointing to the many sights along the turn of the river.

Traffic now nearly stopped at a standstill, she turned right onto W Huron Avenue and parked. Happy to arrive early to the restaurant, she added their name to the waiting list. The Lost Dog Café was one of her father's favorite places to enjoy a chat over breakfast. A creature of habit, he always ordered the same thing: Folly Benedict: English muffin topped with a crab cake, a shrimp cake, poached eggs and hollandaise sauce. With so many choices, it was hard for Victoria to decide between the shrimp and grits or the homemade chicken salad croissant. She ordered the salted caramel coffee then noticed this morning's special: "What's your quiche of the day?"

"We have two: the veggie and the meat quiche. It comes with cheese grits and fresh fruit."

"That sounds perfect. I'll have the veggie quiche."

Her father studied her face. He kept staring deep into her eyes until she became uncomfortable.

"What is it, Daddy?"

"I have to know the truth. I've been waiting all these years for you to tell me about Megan. Are you responsible?"

"Why would you think that I'm responsible?" Victoria's face showed her surprise for a split second, "Meg and I were best friends. I loved her!" Her face contorted into the look of a sweet innocent child.

Dr. Bennett adjusted himself in his chair, he leaned forward and took his daughter's hand and held it. Patiently he waited until Victoria met his gaze. "Victoria, I remember how upset you were when it became evident that Meg and Guy were becoming closer." Attempting to look away, her father's eyes wouldn't allow it. Still holding her hand, "I do remember that you loved Megan. But I also remember your jealousy of her relationship with Guy."

"Yes, I was jealous. Megan! Megan! Megan! It became all about Megan! I couldn't take it anymore! She had stolen MY life! I had to share everything! My father! My honor as valedictorian was stolen!! She stole my future husband, Guy. So, I did something about it."

"I thought so. But I really didn't want to know. Didn't want to admit that my little girl is a murderer."

He looked up at Victoria.

"Oh! Daddy! Don't be so dramatic." Leaning forward, Victoria whispered, "I didn't murder her, I paid someone else to do it."

Neither of them spoke for the rest of breakfast. Afterwards they meandered outside as if the conversation had never happened.

Victoria and her father were sitting on the bench, in the memorial garden behind the community center. She was still sipping on her cup of coffee from the Lost Dog Café when Brooke and Corely approached the pair and stood in front of them.

"Victoria Bennett, you are under arrest for the murder of Megan Taylor. You have the right to remain silent. Anything you say can and will be used against you in a court of law. You have the right to an attorney. If you cannot afford an attorney, one will be appointed for you."

32 CLOSE THE LOOPS

Victoria Bennett was convicted of solicitation of murder and was sentenced to the maximum of 20 years. Her fingerprints were found on the Mountain Dew bottle which contained narcotics. Victoria was also convicted of attempted murder of Murphy Wainwright and received an additional 15 years non-concurrent.

Murphy Wainwright took a plea deal and was sentenced to 20 years. The Sea Turtle Foundation on Folly continues to thrive. Donations and Volunteers are always needed to care for the beach.

Dr. Raymond Bennett continues to live on Folly. He does not leave the island, still shops at Berts and prefers to remember Victoria as a child.

Janice and Dr. Bob Bathe were absolved of any wrongdoing and continue to enjoy the arts together.

Palmer had his total knee replacement. He is recovering well and continues to use his index fingers to type.

All those years ago, Megan floated face down in the surf, she felt at peace. Just peace, no pain, no suffering from the surfboard leash. Although she had always believed the ocean to be her home, Megan had been wrong. She also realized that the mistake was forgiven as her Maker called Megan to her true Home.

WASHED AWAY

ABOUT THE AUTHOR

Vanna Byrd is a beachside mystery author who enjoys seeing your pictures of the beach on her author page. She grew up in rural Red Bank Creek, SC where her imagination was allowed to flourish. Today, she loves to explore the coastal wildlife with her daughter and dance to live music with her husband of over 20 years.

WASHED AWAY LOCATIONS

Folly Beach, South Carolina
https://visitfolly.com/

Live Cam and Surf Report
https://www.oceansurfshop.com/

https://www.surfline.com/surf-report/washout/5842041f4e65fad6a7708a85

Bowen's Island Restaurant
https://bowensisland.com/

Bert's Market
https://bertsmarket.com/

Folly Beach Crab Shack
https://www.crabshacks.com/folly-beach.php

Tides Folly Beach
https://www.tidesfollybeach.com/

California Dreaming
https://californiadreaming.rest/location/Charleston-SC/

Marina Variety Store
https://www.varietystorerestaurant.com/

Charleston County Park on Folly Island
https://www.ccprc.com/61/Folly-Beach-County-Park

City of Folly Beach Park on Folly Island
https://cityoffollybeach.com/folly-beach-parks

Folly Sol
https://folly-sol.square.site/

Folly Beach Pier
https://ccprc.com/1753/Folly-Beach-Pier

Morris Island Lighthouse
https://www.ccprc.com/3149/Lighthouse-Inlet-Heritage-Preserve

The Lost Dog Cafe, Folly Beach
https://lostdogfollybeach.com/

FACEBOOK

Lickety Pop Balloon Shop
Toby Turtle
I Love Folly Beach SC
Folly History Walk
Vanna Byrd

BOOKS IN THIS SERIES

The Tidal Detective

Your vacation just became a mystery. Readers experience a novella length, "weekend mystery" created around the setting of a local beach town. Visit the crime scene, walk the beach from Brooke's point of view or stroll the inspired scenes for the mystery. Get to know each character as they reveal insights into the coastal community hangouts, vibe, and etiquette while Detective Brooke Mason Reveals her thoughts as she explores cluse to solve the murder.

BOARDWALKS AND FLIPFLOPS: A KIAWAH ISLAND VACATION MYSTERY

Sunrise breaks across the blue-grey water of the Atlantic Ocean as the sound of waves gently crashing against the light brown beach sand fill the breezy morning air. The thick smell of salt reminds Detective Brooke Mason that tragedy can strike in beautiful places. Kiawah Island a luxurious South Carolina sea island community where the relaxing resort lifestyle is suddenly replaced by the reality of a suspicious death. Immerse yourself into the roundabout world of Boardwalks and FlipFlops questioning each suspect until the very end.

The first mystery in the Tidal Detective Series, told through the eyes of Kathleen Rothwell and Lauren Wright, 36-year-old long lost friends, one of whom is the possible victim of foul play. Along with Officer Brooke Mason, a 28-year-old detective with the MAIT (Major Accident Investigation Team) who is on a mission to solve the case to become a lead homicide investigator in Charleston County. This mystery is intended to be a fun travel companion for a weekend visitor to Kiawah Island.

Made in the USA
Columbia, SC
01 September 2024

40907927R00098